NALANNI **5**

ISBN-13:978-0615774398
ISBN-10:0615774393

Published by Ink Walk Book Publishing, Woodland Hills, CA 91367

www.inkwalk.com

On the evening of August 27, 2005 a female child was born. A child that will be put to the test to save mankind. An unexpected life force will try to keep her from fulfilling her purpose here on earth. An alternate life force from another galaxy that is so diabolically greedy and looking for a chance to take over the earth, enslave mankind, and rob the earth of all its natural resources. Only one thing stands in their way, "NALANNI"! Nalanni is a child that has inherited special powers unbeknown to her father Keith Langdon of Los Angeles, Ca.

On the day of his daughter's 5th birthday their lives start too changed forever.

On the night that Nalanni was born strange things were happening all over the world. There was rain, electrical storms, power outages, and thousands of women were giving birth at the exact same time all over the world. Of all the thousands of children that were born on August 27, 2005 at 4:22pm, Nalanni was the only child to live.

Although Nalanni lived through the ordeal of the complications of her birth, her mother Nakol did not have the same fortune. Nakol gave her life so that Nalanni may live. She knew that Nalanni's life would be important to her family, the world, and all of mankind.

Chapter 1

The Birth

I ran through the house nervously and excited, making sure I wasn't forgetting anything. My wife Nakol was screaming loudly at me, telling me to hurry up and that my baby girl was coming. Hearing her crying out while I was running through the house with an overnight bag in one hand and reaching for my keys with the other, I stumbled over an ottoman. I had been watching television and resting my feet on it while waiting for this moment. I looked upstairs as my wife let out a loud scream, "She's coming!" I quickly ran upstairs to get my wife. Our oldest daughter Paris was at a neighbor's house. Thank God I had already put Nakol's suitcase in the car. I drove through the streets of LA quickly. I made sure I didn't drive too fast to avoid being pulled over by police officers. We got to the hospital just in time for our baby girl to be delivered. While I was excitedly nervous, I noticed that everyone on staff was calm, but not because they had been through this several times, but as if they were expecting us. I quickly dismissed the idea because I thought I was being paranoid. The excitement of my baby being born and not wanting anything to go wrong had me feeling anxious. The doctor quickly tries to put me at ease saying, "The baby will be fine." I was quickly relieved as I followed a nurse that had been trying to get me to calm down and clean up so that I can witness the birth of my baby girl. We had already known what we were having because Nakol had some complications early in the pregnancy. Several tests had revealed the gender of our child. This was our second child, and we were planning to have a couple more.

In the delivery room all the nurses were watching me as if something was wrong. My nervousness resurfaced. I was starting to sweat. I asked the doctor, "What's going on, is everything alright"? While my wife looks to be in excruciating pain the doctor explains the situation. "Your wife's blood pressure is dropping and she's in pain and we don't know why. A person's blood pressure usually rises when they are in pain. It should not be dropping. We are doing everything we can to find out why this is happening and to stabilize her but nothing is working. At this point both their lives are in danger. We may only be able to save one of them."

Nakol looked at me with tears in her eyes. The look on her face brought skin tingling fear into my heart instantly. She told me no matter what, make sure our baby is alright as if she knew she wouldn't make it through the delivery.

"Stop talking like that!" I said as my heart pounded like a base drum.

"Listen to me! Our baby will need you. Make sure you take special care of her because she's special," she said with great urgency.

"I know she's special, she's my little angel."

"No, she's really special. You will see."

Not knowing what she meant, I held her hand and agreed with all my heart to take care of her and her older sister Paris.

I said, "Ok I'll take special care of her" and I held her hand firmly. There was solemn quiet in the delivery room.

Suddenly the monitors start making loud beeping sounds. A nurse quickly comes over and asks me to leave the delivery room. I felt confused, nervous, and scared.

"Come on Mr. Langdon you have to leave so we can save the baby."

"No! I'm not leaving! My wife and baby are in here!"

"You have to get out so we can try to save them both!"

As the nurse finally gets me to leave, I look at Nakol knowing in my heart that this will be the last time I would see her alive. I watched her all the way through doors, as I backed out the room slowly.

I was escorted to a nearby waiting room

where a dark, handsome, medium built, black man wearing a dark blue polo shirt and jeans sat waiting. He had a tan overcoat laid across his lap as if he were expecting bad weather. During the last couple of days they weather has been fairly warm, like in the low eighties. They looked to be about 50 years old and in good physical shape.

I slowly enter the waiting room, checking out the man with my every step. As I sat down across the room from the man, he looks up at me and says, "She'll be alright". Not thinking about what the man had just said, I say, "Yeah, it didn't seem that way. They rushed me out of the delivery room so quick when the monitors started going crazy and making all kinds of noise." The man came over and introduced himself.

"Hi, I'm James Harris, but people call me Jay."

"Hey, pleased to meet you, I'm Keith, Keith Langdon".

"Tuff night huh?"

"You have no idea." (shaking my head)

"Is this your first child?"

Cupping my face in my hands I say, "No. My second and last with my wife." as I started to sob.

"My daughter Paris is six years old. She looks just likes her mother." Thinking about my wife Nakol, I broke down to the floor crying. I held my face as if I couldn't believe these events were really happening. I sat up on the chair and said, "God, why is this happening to me?"

James Harris looked at me and said, "Sometimes Keith, things happen for reasons that we can't or don't want to understand." Hearing his bullshit of a way he chose to comfort me, I say with extreme anger or rage, "Are you trying to fucking tell me that my wife and kid are in there fighting for their lives for some cosmic reason that I will never understand!? What reason would there be to take away my wife and kid?"

"One day you'll understand."

"Excuse me, but I don't think I'll ever understand losing either of them!"

Understanding why my family is being sent through this pain is something I will never understand.

I looked around at the blue-ish gray painted walls and wondered, why did they paint them that color? I know there are psychological reasons that certain colors are chosen for the walls of medical and mental institutions. I thought for a brief minute it must be working because I was thinking about the color of the walls instead of my wife and kid. It didn't last for long though, because my mind quickly went back to them as my anger and sorrow returned. Visions of what could have been, danced around in head. James Harris didn't move an inch, or say another word. He just sat there, across from me in the waiting room of UCLA Harbor Medical Center.

At 4:22pm Nakol delivered a healthy baby girl. I witnessed the birth of Nalanni just as I witnessed Paris' birth. Watching your children being born creates a special bond between you and the children being born and gives you an added respect for the mother. There is nothing like it. The news about Nalanni's birth spread throughout the hospital quickly.
The birth of the child had taken its toll on Nakol. Her body was shutting down. The doctors scrambled to save her but there was nothing more they could do for her. Several attempts were made to save her but she was not responding to the staff's efforts. The monitor made a steady beep, the screen flat lined, and my wife Nakol was dead. Nakol passed away at 4:23pm. My life would never be the same. I loved her. I really loved her.

The doctor comes into the waiting room and informs me that I was the proud father of a 7lb 6oz baby girl.
"What about my wife"?
"We did all that we could to save her."
Tears streamed down my face as my heart

crashed to the deep abyss of my gut.

While sobbing heavily, I looked up at the doctor and ask, "When can I see them"?

Feeling crushed by the fact that I was just informed about my wife's death during delivery, I didn't know what to expect or even do when I saw her. A nurse came in after the Doctor spoke to me about my wife's death. She greeted me with words of comfort and sorrow. With hopes that those words would somehow console me, she spat them out at me ease as if she plenty of time to practice them.

I entered a room full of babies. A nurse brings over a bundle to me. I took one look at her and start to cry once again. "She looks like her mother also. I'm going to name her Nalanni." My wife and I had discussed the name of the child before. We had spent countless hours discussing her name while lying in bed on several occasions. All I could do was stare at my newly born child.

After spending several minutes with my daughter I handed her back to the nurse for feeding. I took one more look at her and I knew that we would be alright. But what I didn't know is that tonight's events are just the beginning of a rough journey that we will never forget and the fate of the world as we knew it rest in our hands.

Walking pass the viewing window were several people crying. Most stopped for a few seconds to look into the nursery. Since there were so many, I thought a family member had just lost a child at birth. I asked the nurse that was attending Nalanni, "What's going on with the people in the hall?"

She said, "You are a lucky man Mr. Langdon."

I gave the nurse a crazy look and said, "What the hell are you talking about? I do have beautiful baby girl, but I lost my wife!"

In the hall way, outside the nursery, several doctors and nurses gathered. Among them was James Harris. They all looked into the viewing window of the nursery towards Nalanni. I turn and look towards Nalanni, and when I turn back to the viewing window several doctors and nurses stood there. James Harris was gone.

One of the doctor's gestures for me to come out into the hall. I hesitate for a second then proceed out into the hall where all the other doctors and nurses are standing. The doctor tells me that I am the luckiest man in the world right now.

I ask him, "Why is everybody saying that?"

He says, "Because so far, your child is the only child to survive out of all the thousands of children that were born at 4:22pm."

"Like I said, Lucky!"

All the attention quickly left me and was directed towards Nalanni. There were whispers of how Nalanni was the special one.

I took a seat in the nearby lobby. A television was on. The news reporting how several children died during birth all over California, then other cities, states, and countries reported the same tragedies were happening where they were. My heart rate started to speed up, I felt nauseated. I thought about making it to a restroom but only made it as far as the nearest trash can. Besides I didn't want to go too far away from the nursery. I raised my head from the trash can to see a nurse and a doctor standing there with me.

"Mr. Langdon you need to calm down." the doctor said in a calm voice. Your daughter is healthy. She'll be fine. I managed to calm down and took my daughter home two days later.

Over the next five years I would go on to see my daughter do extraordinary things that will not register in my mind until her 5th birthday.

Five years have passed and they have kept a close look on her, watching her and our family. They knew how important she will be to mankind and have stayed close to Nalanni, Paris and, myself insuring our safety.

James Harris and his associates weren't the

only ones interested in Nalanni. She is being sought after by beings not from our world. But they have one snag in their pursuit of Nalanni. They don't know who she is. They only know that she exist here on earth and that she is the only thing that can stop them from a plan so diabolical and vicious, the human race would be devastated forever.

Mankind does not know the extent of the events to come but will soon find out in a way that will keep them questioning their strength and unity as a race.

Chapter 2

The Restaurant

It's Friday evening. Paris, Nalanni, and I are sitting down to eat at Nolan's. Nolan's is our favorite restaurant. It's located just a mile or so from our home in Los Angeles. We eat out there every other week as a family ritual. The cozy little restaurant had been chosen by my wife when she was pregnant with Nalanni. I decided to continue to continue to eat there as a family ritual to hold on to old memories and to create new ones for me and the girls.

I ordered my usual, T-bone steak, medium well, eggs scrambled soft, and home style potatoes. Paris and Nalanni both had not decided on their evening meals. We all had raspberry lemon-aid to drink. The restaurant was fairly busy but we managed to secure a booth at the back of the restaurant right across from the kitchen with a good view of a television. There are several pictures of celebrities on the walls that have come here to eat and have their pictures taken with the owners.
It was 8:00pm and House was on television.

House is one of my favorite shows. Other families were interested in the TV show also.

Paris asks, "So dad what are we doing this weekend?"
"I don't know, it depends on what Nalanni wants to do. It's her birthday."
"I wanna go to Disneyland".
A couple next to us hears our conversation and looks over and wishes Nalanni happy birthday. "How old are you sweetie?" The woman asks.
"I'm four but I'm gonna be five on my birthday." she says with a smile.
"Yeah, four going on 15", says Paris.

"No I'm not. Daddy, tell Paris to stop saying that about me".

"Paris your sister is an angel" I say sarcastically.

"Yeah right. Whatever dad".

"Come on girls look at the menus and see what you want".

"Daddy I don't know what I want. Let Nalanni go first".

"I know what I want. I want pancakes and bacon".

"She always gets the same thing".

"That's because she knows what she wants."

"Ok, I know what I want now".

"About time".

"I want the chicken strips and fries with barbeque sauce".

Nalanni and I always have breakfast for dinner.

Nalanni age 2 The first sign *(flash back)*

I was out in the backyard tending to my Birmingham Roller Pigeons. Paris was at school and Nalanni was right outside of my pigeon loft playing in the grass. She noticed a red and white badge pigeon under the kit box, which is a cage used for flying my roller pigeons. She said, "Daddy look, a bird."
"What bird?" I asked.
"The one right there on da ground", said the toddler.
I stepped out of my pigeon loft and looked to my left to see a pigeon on the ground that had been missing since yesterday morning. A falcon had chased and caught it during an early morning flight.

I thought that bird was dead because I saw it get caught by a female peregrine falcon. It had apparently escaped the falcon's strong sharp talons. I noticed it had been cut on the breast about 3 inches down its breast when I picked it up to examine it. The pigeon didn't look like it was going to make it, so I put it in the exhibition coop and went back inside the loft.

When I went back inside the loft Nalanni went over and talked to the bird.

Lil bird got an owie. It's gonna be ok birdie. She reached into the cage to touch the bird. She touched the bird and said, "All better now".

I came out of the loft, looked at my watch. It was 2:30pm. It was time to go pick up Paris from school. I loaded Nalanni into the car seat and off we went to pick up her big sister.

We pulled up in front of La Belle Elementary School. Paris was already waiting for us in front. We got there a few minutes later than normal.

Dad, what took yal so long?

"I had to finish feeding the birds so I could cook dinner when we get home".

"Oh, okay".

"Paris, daddy's bird was hurt and I fixed it for him".

"Daddy what is she talking about"?

"I have no idea what she's talking about".

"I fixed it. I did. I did. Yal don't believe

me".
"I believe you baby".
"Thank you daddy."
"How did you fix the bird?"
"I fixed his owie?"
"Oh thank you baby", I said to help keep her enthused.

The next day when I went in the backyard to the loft, I didn't notice the hurt bird in the exhibition coop. I let out a kit of rollers. I walked around the kit box and noticed that the hurt bird was looking better. I picked up the bird to examine it. To my surprise I could not find the wound on the bird. I continued to look with astonishment. I thought about what Nalanni had said, "*I fixed it for you daddy*". I shook my head and thought maybe I had made a mistake when diagnosing the bird the previous day and quickly dismissed what Nalanni had said.
There was dried blood on the bird but no wound.
As I finished feeding my pigeons, I couldn't stop thinking about what happened with the pigeon earlier. I knew what I had seen. The bird was cut on the breast and part of the crop was open. I kept playing the scene over and over in my mind. The picture is surely clear in my head. The bird was definitely injured!

On the television there was an amber alert.
"Turn that up please", I asked the waitress.
The news was on the television. Channel 4
Eye Witness News was reporting the
ongoing abductions of children.
"*Another child was reported missing this
evening at 5:15pm. This makes the 13th child
in a span of 3 weeks. This child was
reported missing in Inglewood. The child
was a 5 year old boy, taken from his mother
at a gas station on La Cienega and
Florence. The child was snatched right out
of the mother's car while she was paying for
her gas*".

All around the city of Los Angeles there
were complaints of children coming up
missing. Boys and girls around the age of 5
are missing all over LA.
I was focusing and listening to the news, and
I turned my head towards my girls, raised
my eyebrows, and shook my head as if to
say with my mind, I won't let whoever is
doing this get my girls. With the news still
playing in the background, I tell my
daughters, "That is why we must always be
careful and stay close to each other and you
girls should never talk to strangers. There
are some crazy people out there".
"Daddy you not gonna let those bad people
get us huh", says Nalanni.

"Girl aint nobody gonna get us", said Paris.

"I'm not going to let anything happen to you girls".

Although I would give my life to save my daughters, I feel that one of them may be in danger, a target for the abductors that were terrorizing LA's children. I knew in my heart that I needed to keep a close eye on my 5 year old daughter.

The comment her mother made before she died came to mind. *"Take care of our baby she special."*

Chapter 3

The waitress returned to our table with the food. She remembered our orders to the tee. The girls were glad the food had arrived at the table.

"I'm glad the food is here because I'm hungry", said Paris.

"Me too," said Nalanni.

"You are always hungry", said Paris.

"Ok, ok girls. Stop fussing and eat your food", I said.

As we were sitting there about to eat our dinner, the lights flickered, the temperature in the restaurant seemed to drop twenty degrees in a matter of seconds, and the building started to shake a bit. People starting screaming, Earth Quake, Earth Quake!

Nalanni and Paris both complained about being cold.

What I saw then would make any person doubt their sanity.

There were two children sitting with their parents. There was a boy and a little girl there having dinner with their parents. Both children were frightened. The parents were trying desperately to keep the kids calm.

There were dishes breaking in the kitchen and people were starting to get frightened. You could hear screams coming from all over the restaurant. I myself was starting to wonder what was going on. This could not be a normal earthquake. It was lasting too long and was steady. Then suddenly a loud hum seemed to be coming from the ceiling of the restaurant as if there was someone or something trying to literally come down through the roof. All the patrons looked up towards the ceiling. Fear was on the faces of all the people in the restaurant. The temperature dropped to about freezing. While all of this was happening, I slowly got up and told my daughters to get up. Speaking in a medium toned voice, I told them to get up because we needed to go. Although I was up with my daughters and moving towards the kitchen area. No one noticed me and my family exiting the dining area of the restaurant. I burst through the kitchen door and the workers were not concerned about me coming in. Their main concern was all the excitement that was going on inside the restaurant. I could hear the screams becoming more intense as if filled with terror. I turned and looked behind me through the kitchen doors. What I saw made me freeze in my tracks for a couple seconds. I couldn't grasp what I had just seen. I almost took a step back inside the restaurant when I saw one of the boys from the family that was sitting near us vanish and reappear right before my eyes. The young boy had just vanished into thin air and come back within a fraction of a second. He had been the younger of the two children. He was probably the same age as Nalanni. I quickly turned back around, picked up Nalanni, told Paris to hurry, and ran through the kitchen. Paris and Nalanni were scared as we ran through the kitchen. A man that was a kitchen worker came out of the freezer as we ran past. I gave him a shoulder thrust as if trying to block for a running back I was assigned to protect. The man, a short Hispanic man, went flying into a rack of pots and pans. He hit the rack with a loud crash as several pots and pans fell all over the floor. As I continued to make my way through the kitchen I could still hear the screams and the humming coming from behind me. My mind kept taking me back to the image of the boy vanishing as I crashed through the kitchen knocking down everyone and everything in my way as I made the way clear for me and my girls to get out of the restaurant. I could now see the exit. It was no more than ten feet from me. I got to the door and peaked out to see what was going on outside the restaurant. I was amazed to see that everything looked normal, as if the whole word was oblivious to what was taking place inside the restaurant. I thought to myself, what the hell is going on? I saw people walking around going about their day like normal, and inside the restaurant is total chaos. The screams were still coming from behind me. I just stepped out of the restaurant and closed the door. I didn't know what the hell was going on. The one thing I did know was that the girls and I are safe, at least for now.

Chapter 4

Nalanni age 3, "The Crash" (*the second sign)*

Driving home from Lancaster, CA down the 14fwy, traffic was light. Michael Jackson's Thriller was playing on the radio. We were singing to it. Paris was in the front passenger seat and Nalanni was in the back in her car seat. They were trying to mimic the dance sequences while sitting in their seats. I joined in on the parts I knew, or thought I knew.

My mind kept wondering what life would be like had my wife Nakol survived the birth along with Nalanni. I loved my wife dearly. I see my wife in my daughters but in different ways with each child. Paris has her mother's green eyes and Nalanni has her golden brown smooth skin. I often wished she could have met Nalanni and seen how much Paris has grown and how much of a young woman she is at age twelve.

Just as I snapped out of my short Trans, a blue SUV swerved into a Mercedes Benz. I was driving in the center lane. The SUV swerved from right to left striking the Benz on the driver side door. The Benz spun around a couple of times before flipping over on the passenger side and rolling down the side of the road into a ditch. The Benz landed upside down in the ditch. The driver looked to be in serious pain. I pulled over to check and see if the man was alright. The SUV sustained minimal damage and the driver seemed to be just shook up at worst. I told the girls to stay in the car while I check on the man in the Benz. As I approached the vehicle I could hear the man moaning. When I got a visual on the man, I could see that the man appeared to be hurt very badly. A metal object seemed to have pierced his chest. He was having a hard time breathing. I yelled to a female motorist that was coming over to assist, to call 911. She said she had already called 911 and an ambulance is on the way. The car was smoking profusely. I could smell gas. Knowing that I was not suppose to move a trauma victim I knew I needed to get this man out of the car quickly. I went around to the driver's side of the car. Lookie-loos had traffic slowed down and backed up for miles already. It's only been a few minutes since the accident happened. When I walked around the back of the car, I saw it had caught on fire. I got the man loose and pulled him from the car. I knew I was not supposed to move him but the car might explode. When I got the man to the side of the freeway, the man appeared to be slipping away. I felt a small hand touch my right shoulder. It was Nalanni. I told her to go back to the car.

She said, "Daddy I can help".

I told her, "there is nothing that u can do baby, so go back to the car".

Paris comes over and says, "Dad I told her not to get out of the car but she don't listen to me".

While I was talking to Paris, Nalanni went over to the man. She whispered to the man, "I'm gonna fix it for you ok"?

The man looked at her as if he was looking at an angel. He looked into her eyes. And as he did, he knew he would be alright.

I turned around and saw Nalanni leaning over the man. I quickly ran over to where Nalanni and the man were. Nalanni's back was to me. As I got closer I could see that the man appeared to be focused on Nalanni.

When I saw Nalanni's hands, I started to panic. Nalanni's hands were covered in blood. The blood from the man didn't seem to bother her at all. That much blood would have freaked the average 5 year old kid out. Nalanni was calm and whispering to the man. I could not make out what she was saying. Nalanni was holding the man's left hand in her right hand now. What Nalanni

did next shocked me. Again I thought I was
seeing things. I thought maybe I was
tripping from all of the excitement. Things
like that can't happen, at least not in real
life.
The child and the man were shielded from
the motorist passing by. They were all trying
to see what was going on. A crowd was
forming behind me, but no one was close
enough to see what was going on behind the
wrecked car. Some stayed away in fear of
the car exploding.
Behind the wreckage Nalanni had done the
unthinkable. She had defied physics as we
knew it.
With the car smoking and the sirens from
the emergency vehicles getting closer, she
took her left hand, grabbed the metal object
and as she pulled it from the man's chest,
she leaned in closer to him as if to be
whispering. She whispered the words,
*"Everything will be alright. I fixed it for
you"* to the man again. Nalanni had just
healed a man with a metal object impaled in
his chest.
The emergency vehicles had arrived. They
approached the man quickly from the west
which was the front of the wrecked vehicle.
Three paramedics attended to the wounded
man while the fire fighters checked on the
smoking car.
I was still trying to grasp what I had just
seen. Nalanni had just healed a man before

my eyes. In my mind I was trying rationalize what I had just seen. I thought maybe the man was not hurt badly at all. That metal spike was not actually pierced that deep inside the man's chest I thought. I was so deep in thought I could not hear the paramedic calling out to me, asking me, "Whose child is this? We need this child away from here."

(restaurant scene continued)
My heart was racing as I entered the parking lot of the restaurant. All I could think of as I jogged with Nalanni in my arms and Paris at my side was what the hell is going on here? I wondered if this had all been a bad dream and maybe I was going to awaken soon. The parking lot appeared to be normal. I noticed a man watching me and my daughters. I thought I recognized the man, but couldn't remember where I had met him. I looked to see where I had parked the vehicle. There it is I thought as I saw my black, 1975 Blazer. I turned around to see if we were still being watched. There was no one there watching us.

Chapter 5

We arrived at our house in Los Angeles at 10:13pm. The house was an old house built in the 1930's. It was a 3 bedroom, 1 ¼ bath house with a large kitchen that faced the street in the south direction. We had moved back here after Nakol's death. There were too many memories for me and Paris at the other house. This house had been left to me by my mother seven years ago when she passed away from C.O.P.D. (*Chronic Obstruction Pulmonary Disease*). I hadn't done anything with the house until my wife's death. I had done some minor changes to the house. I painted the house a sort of light avocado green with white trimming. I cut the trees from the driveway, put in new carpet, and painted the whole interior of the house an eggshell white, except the girl's room.

I instructed the girls to take baths as I decided to make some calls to see if anybody I knew heard anything about the restaurant.

I called my brother Damon first and told him I need to talk to him in person. Damon is my younger brother. Damon and I had always been close. Although Damon is 12 years younger than me, we've always been close. Damon and I had been hustlers together when we were younger. I taught Damon the ways of the street and how to survive out there. Damon just never left the street life.

I called my best friend Marcus just to hear my best friend's familiar voice and to make sure he and his kids were alright. As always they were fine. Their oldest daughter Britney will be graduating from high school soon and they are excited about that. I wanted to tell Marcus what had transpired over the last three or four hours but didn't know how to tell him in fear of how it would sound. I decide not to say anything yet or at least until I figured a few things out. Sitting there in sort of a daze, I wondered how this could be happening. I thought for a moment that I was being punk'd, but no celebrity popped out with a friend of mine. Besides, the scenarios had been to elaborate to pull off with such detail. Not wanting to get more confused, I just put the events to the back of my mind and went to check on the girls.

I called out and asked if the girls were finished bathing. I heard Nalanni say, "Yeah daddy we're finished". A few minutes later the bathroom door opens. The girls come out with towels rapped around them. "Dad, what are we going to wear" Says Paris. I thought for a min and said, "Let's see what we can find in here clean".

I had not done laundry yet but I had always kept clean clothes in the hallway closet for Paris and Nalanni. When Paris was a small girl I kept spare clothes in here just in case. Those clothes were too small for Paris but should fit Nalanni. I found a couple of old gowns that my wife used to wear. She just had to wear them until I was able to wash some clean clothes for them. I told Paris to try one on. Paris asked me where I got the gowns. I told her, they had belonged to her mother. Wow! These belonged to mom? She was glad to be able to wear a gown that belonged to her mother.

"I want to wear one too", said Nalanni.

I told Nalanni that she could wear the other one. I told the girls to put on the gowns and I would be in to tuck them in.

Ten minutes later I walked down the hall and tapped on the door to the room the girls were in. I heard the girls inside giggling. "Is it safe to come in", he asked? Two voices simultaneously said, "Yes". As I entered the room I noticed the bed to his left was empty.

Both girls were in the full size bed. They had decided to sleep together.

"I guess I have to tuck you both in at the same time", I said to the girls.

"Well, I guess you do", said Paris.

I pulled the covers up over the girls. I then leaned over and kissed both girls on the forehead. I kissed Nalanni first then Paris. I told Paris that I was proud of her for being so brave during our ordeal. Paris asked me had happened. I told her it was an earthquake and we had to get out of the restaurant quickly. Nalanni said, "Daddy I'm hungry. We didn't get a chance to eat our food."

I said, "That's right."

With all of the excitement I forgot they didn't get a chance to finish their dinner. Actually they didn't really get to start eating. I went in the kitchen and popped a few corndogs in the microwave oven. I gave them some fruit and juice with the corndogs. They sat in the kitchen table, ate their short meals, and then I put them to bed for the second time.

Their room is painted a soft pastel pink. The carpet is almost the same color but the difference in texture makes the carpet look slightly darker. These are the colors that they both agreed on. There is a twin bed and a full sized bed in their room. Over the twin bed there is a few of Nalanni's drawings on the wall. Over the full size bed is a picture of Paris at one of her cheerleading events. Photo was her doing one of her award winning jumps.

I told the girls it's time to try this again. They both got in the bed again. I kissed them on the forehead again, in the same order as before, Nalanni then Paris. Paris smiled and then closed her eyes and went to sleep.

Nalanni was still awake. She watched as I walked out of the bedroom. Even with everything that has been going on, Nalanni seemed to not be rattled, as if she knew something about the events taking place. She knew I loved her and her sister. She also knew I wouldn't be with them forever. She knew that I would soon be away from them. She just didn't know when.

After I tucked the girls in I headed into the kitchen to make me a cup of coffee. It was remarkable how everything had remained the same. Mint green walls and drawer trim were a good idea. The green marble counter tops were the finishing touch to the white cabinets. After the 2nd cup of coffee my mind was whizzing around, replaying all the events that occurred over the past three years. The restaurant event is planted in the forefront of my memories. I sat there at the white kitchen table, pondering, what are they after, and why does it seem as if Nalanni is the key? I took another sip of my coffee then grabbed the remote and turned on the television. I was not surprised when I saw they were reporting about the restaurant incident. The news reporter talked about a man running out of the restaurant and not paying for his family's meal.

They reported that a man went crazy, refused to pay for his family's meals, and ran out of the restaurant through the kitchen. The disappearing children were never mentioned. I know what I saw in that restaurant. My girls didn't actually see anything. I had grabbed them up and ran before it happened.

Was I imagining all this? Was this all just happening in my mind? What's more important is will it happen again? I put my hands on my face, rubbed my temples, and shook my head as if trying to shake my mind free of all these events. I decided I needed something a little stronger to drink. I looked into a small cabinet just above the refrigerator. A half-filled bottle of Hennessey. I got a glass from the cabinet and poured myself a drink. Then another and another and another. By the third drink I was starting to forget the events of the day. Now I am drunk.

After I walked out of the room Nalanni whispers Paris' name to see if she was asleep. Paris answers her to let her know that she was not asleep. Nalanni explains to Paris how she need to be strong through all that was about to happen. Paris asks Nalanni, "How did you learn to speak to me that way?

"I don't know. It just happened. I thought about saying something to you without someone hearing me and it just happened."

"You mean like at Nolan's."

"Yeah."

"Nalanni, are you scared?"

"I was scared at first, then mommy told me I gotta try and not be scared for everybody."

"You can't be scared either Paris. We're going to need you too."

"How did you talk to mommy?"

"I didn't say I talked to mommy. I said she talked to me."

"But how did you know it was her? She died giving birth to you."

"I know her voice. She used to talk to me all the time when I was in her stomach."

With tears rolling down her face Paris says, "I really miss her."

Nalanni says, "Don't cry Paris. She is with us all the time, even now."

Just then Paris felt a cool breeze pass through her. The breeze sent a pleasant chill down to her spine. Just then she saw a silhouette of mother's face. Her smiling face soothed her as the image briefly passes through her mind. Paris smiles and starts to cry again.

"Why are you crying?" asked Nalanni.

"I saw her and felt her. It felt like she was a

part of me. She reassured me that everything was really going to be alright. I really miss her." said Paris.

I know you do sister. But like mommy said, "We are going to be alright."

Nalanni gets out of her bed and climbs in the bed with Paris. Paris throws the cover over Nalanni, they cuddle up together like the loving sisters they are and fall asleep.

Chapter 6

Damon pulled into the gas station on Florence and Normandie. It was 2am and the gas station was pretty much quiet except for a few crack heads waiting by the pumps, hoping they can pump gas to hustle up enough money to buy more crack.

As he got out of his 850 BMW on 24" rims, a crack head asked him if he could pump his gas for some change. Damon said, in a stern voice, "Nawl man I got this." The man asked again, "Come on sir can I please pump yo gas"?

Damon now getting a little frustrated pulled back one side of his dark blue button up shirt at the waste brandishing his nickel plated Smith & Wesson 10mm. He then told the man which seem to appear out of nowhere, to back the fuck up. Damon started to wonder where the man had come from.

He asked the man, "Where in the fuck did you come from any way? I didn't see you when I pulled in this mutha fucka"! The man calmly told Damon, "Relax Damon, you're going to need all of that aggression for something bigger and more dangerous than just me."

"How the fuck do you know my name? Who the hell are you?!"

The man said, "Who I am is not important right now. You should go to your brother Keith, he's going to need you. The girl is the key to everything."

"What girl?", said Damon?

"The only girl that matters right now", said the man.

"Now go to the house at 1851 w 83rd street. Your brother Keith is there. He's gonna need you".

"How the hell do you know so much about us cuz? Who the fuck are you?! (*Yelling*)

"I'm a friend. Now go to your brother".

Feeling confused, Damon slowly lowers his gun and backs away.

Damon gets into his car and immediately picks up his phone to call me. He's driving fast and dialing the number. I do not answer the phone. He tries to call the land line but there is no answer. He speeds down Normandie Avenue doing around 60 mph. He turns right on 83rd street heading west towards Western Avenue. He runs right through the light on Denker Ave. He slows down at Western only because of the large dips at that intersection. He pulls up to the house to see that my blazer is parked in the driveway and the kitchen light is on. There were no other lights on in the house. He tries my cell one more time. There was still no answer.

Damon got out of the car, pulled out his gun slowly and approached the dark house. The porch light was not on, which made the yard dark. No light was shining from the moon like some nights when they were young boys. They used to play in the front yard on some summer nights when they were young. As he walked down the drive way, he paid close attention to the shadowed areas of the yard. A large willow tree was in the middle of the front yard. This tree provided shade on hot summer days for us for many years. Now the tree merely provided shelter for someone trying to hurt his brother.

Damon's mind is in full motion trying to figure what is going on.

Is someone trying to hurt my brother? Or is someone after one of the girls? Nalanni is only five years old and Paris is only twelve. Why would anybody want to hurt them? More importantly, who?

He reached the porch without incident. He

walked around the side of the house where the driveway continued to the garage. My blazer truck was parked in front of the garage. The blinds in the kitchen were slightly open, just enough to see me sitting at the kitchen table with my head on the table. He could see a bottle of alcohol on the table almost empty. He walks back around to the front of the house. He approaches the front door and checks it to see if it's locked, and it is. He remembers the spare key is always in the middle flower pot inside a small fake rock. He reaches down to get it and hears something behind him. He flings around quickly to see a possum walking down the side of the brick wall in the driveway. He unlocks the door, goes in and inspects the house. Starting with the living room, he works his way down the hall and checks the bed rooms. He finds the girls sleeping in his mother's old room. They seemed to be alright. He goes into the kitchen and checks on his brother. He puts his gun away and tries to awaken me.

"Damn he's drunk", said Damon.

In all his years, he had never seen me drunk before. He starts to wonder, *what could have driven him to this point?*

Damon tried several times and I would not budge. So Damon decided to get me into the bed. Damon being 5'10" and 240 lbs. had no problem getting me down the hall and into my bed. I'm taller than Damon but I only weigh 210lbs. After getting me in the bed Damon goes into the living room and turns on the television. At this hour there isn't much on TV except infomercials, videos, and religious networks. He got up and made sure the door was locked. He went down the hall and got a blanket and pillow. Before he knew it, he was asleep.

Chapter 7

I was awakened by the sounds of laughter and a loud television. My head was pounding. I had a hangover. I had never had a hangover before because I had never been drunk before. I went to the bathroom, got me a couple Tylenol capsules. I grabbed a bottle of water off the counter, quickly swallowed both capsules, and flushed them down with the whole bottle of water. I thought to myself that I would never drink alcohol like that again. This hangover business was knew to me and I didn't like it. I looked into the mirror in the kitchen and wondered as I looked at my reflection, what the hell were you thinking? My head pounded as I walked to the living room to see what was going on. The girls were up and playing with someone other than each other. The girls were rolling around on the floor, jumping on, and punching my little brother Damon. Nalanni was the first to notice me. She looked up and gave me a smile, and a good morning daddy. Paris soon joined in with her good morning daddy. Damon added a good morning bro. Damon said, "Bro we need to talk"!

He got up off the floor and told the girls he needed to talk to me.

I asked him what was on his mind. He told me about the events of last and his encounter with a strange man. He told me how the man seemed to have known him, me and the girls. He said he didn't get the man's name. He explained how the man seemed to have appeared out of thin air. And how no matter how mad he had gotten, the man remained calm.

It was like his only objective was to get my brother to me.

I told Damon to go into the backyard so we could talk. Damon follow me through the kitchen and out into the backyard. We walked by the small waterfall which was once a small Koi pond and out back to the old lofts. My old pigeon loft was still standing in the backyard. After I had moved my birds to Hacienda Heights, CA, the loft was converted into a workout room. I built a new loft before I moved away and had taken it with me to Hacienda Heights, but moved it back when we moved back after my wife passed away. We walked around the old fish pond that had been damaged during the quakes in the 70's and 80's. We stepped into the workout room. I closed the door behind us. It was dark and very dusty. Cobwebs had formed from the lack of use of the workout room. There were several weight machines, some steel barbells, weight benches, and a treadmill. The carpet was a dirty beige color. An old 24" television sat up on a shelf in a corner. My friends and I had watched several basketball games on that TV. I dusted off one of the benches near the door. Damon sat on the bench of the bow flex that was left of the door. I sat down quiet for a moment until Damon turned to me and said, "What's up bro?"

I said, "You may think I'm crazy, but I've seen some shit that has me thinking I'm crazy."

"What kind of shit?" said Damon?

"The kind of shit people get committed for".

I paused for a minute, took in a deep breath and said, "Man, we were in Nolan's about to eat dinner. Everything was fine. We were talking about our plans for Nalanni's birthday. We had just finished ordering our food. Then all of a sudden the building started shaking, like a small earthquake. Then there was this sound. It was like a humming, vibrating noise. While the shaking and humming was going on, some weirder shit happened. The ceiling sort of like opened up, and these things came through and started taking the children. I mean they made the children disappear in thin air and reappear just as fast. I thought I was really tripping. Then my parental instincts kicked in and I grabbed the girls and got the hell out of there".

Damon lets out a chuckle.

"Man, you must still be drunk", said Damon.

"I am not playing. This shit really happened!" I told him.

Damon asks me am I alright? I told him I was alright except for my hangover and that he needed to believe me. Then I told him, "The strange thing about all of this is, when we got out the restaurant, it was as if nothing had happened. Everything was normal. People were walking around like nothing ever happened. Even the news said that I was a crazy man that ran out the restaurant to avoid paying for his families meals".

I could tell by the look on his face that he didn't believe me. He had this smirk on his face that suggested that very fact. I knew that what I was saying sounded far-fetched, but it was the truth. I asked him to explain what had happened to him at the gas station last night.

He said, "I just pulled into the gas station to get gas and a man seemed to have popped out of nowhere."

"You see, I told you something is going on around here."

"Man, bro, you trippin," he said. The man did seem to have come out of nowhere, but maybe I just didn't see him or something."

"Damon, I'm telling you, something really fucked up is going on around here!"

Chapter 8

Several people were gathered inside the
county building on Jefferson and Figueroa.
It's the end of the month and people are
trying to get their paper work in order so
they can receive their government aid on the
first of the month. People are walking
around pouting and complaining their cash
aid being suspended, cut, or denied.

A little boy about 6 years old is sitting
calmly with his mother. There are several
other children there also but these kids are
getting on their parent's nerves. They're
standing on chairs, chasing each other
around and bumping into people standing in
line.

A woman sitting in the service window
calmly tells one of the parents to get control
of her children. The mother gives the
woman an attitude smirk, as if to say, "fuck
you bitch."

The woman in the service window just

shakes her head and makes a comment under her breath that the mother barely hears. The mother of the child not knowing what she actually said gets mad and says, "Forget you bitch! And walks away from the window.

RUMBLE, RUMBLE, RUMBLE the building starts to vibrate. The six year old boy suddenly looks up towards the 12 foot high ceiling as if something was up there.

Suddenly there was a humming sound in the building. The humming was getting louder and louder as if someone was turning up the volume on an amplifier that was not connected correctly. The people in the building all at once put their hands over their ears trying desperately to keep the sound out of their heads. Then vroommmm! A black hole opened up in the ceiling. At that time all eyes were on the black hole. As the people watched the hole with intrigue and fear, something came down. A cloudy like effervescent like being of a humanoid nature, but with no eyes. Deep black holes were where their eyes should have been. The creatures heads turned quickly towards the children that were playing seconds earlier but now had their hands covering their ears and looking up at them. As they looked towards the kids, each one vanished like a quick fading vapor. Poof, they were gone. For every creature that disappeared so did a child. Each child disappeared with the creatures but reappeared. For every child there was a creature and more.

The 6 year old boy quickly hid under a desk next to the wall where he and his mother were sitting. Then all of a sudden the remaining beings shot up through the hole in the ceiling like smoke being sucked through a vacuum. After the last being went through, the humming stop and the hole closed. Everything stopped. The parents, mostly women stood there as if they had no idea what had just happened. The workers were shaken and confused as well. There were no 911 calls or bursts of panic. Everyone except for the children was left disoriented. This incident was over. But what really happened in the County Building on Jefferson?

Chapter 9

After my talk with Damon I went back into the house to make breakfast for the girls. On the menu was turkey bacon, eggs, grits with butter, cinnamon raisin bagels, orange juice, and or milk.
I set the table for the four of us to eat. Nalanni was the first to enter the kitchen.
"Good morning baby girl,"
"Good morning Daddy".
"Where is your sister?"
"She's coming. You know she gotta comb her hair first."
Paris walks into the kitchen. Everybody at the table greets her with a sarcastic god morning. She simply smiles because she knows everybody was waiting on her so they could eat.
Paris sat down next to Damon. Nalanni made sure she was sitting next to me. I asked everyone to bow their heads so I could say grace. With all heads down I started, "Dear God, we thank you for this meal we are receiving today and that it may nourish our bodies for the start of this wonderful day

you have blessed us with. We also ask that you continue to watch over us (*Paris and Nalanni look at each other wondering when I was going to finish the prayer so they can eat*) as we go through the day. Amen.

"Dang dad we thought you were going to preach a sermon." said Paris. *Nalanni smiles and laughs* .Nalanni has this smile that demands you to smile with her. She still has her baby teeth so the smile suggest that a cute innocence is always present.

What are you laughing at Nalanni? You don't even know what a sermon is.

"So what." said Nalanni.

The girls went back and forth for a few seconds. I politely asked the girls to cut it out and eat their breakfast.

"So what's the plan big bro?"

The television was on in the kitchen. A news flash came on the TV.

Eye witness news was doing a report on an incident that happened at the DPSS building on Jefferson and Figueroa.

They reported that a parent became violent and attacked a social worker for denying her family government aid. When they showed the video tape, for a split second it looked like all the people there were looking up at the ceiling. Then their faces quickly looked forward. I quickly asked Damon, "Did you see that?"

He said, "See what? I didn't see anything."

I grabbed the remote off the kitchen table,

pushed rewind on the DVR functions. I pushed play again. I got to the part where the all the people's faces were facing upward towards the ceiling. They were only in that position for a split second and changed quickly.

I said, "Now did you see that?"

Damon said, "Yeah, so. That doesn't mean anything. Bro stop trippin."

I said, "Look, I'm not trippin."

I showed Damon the recording a couple more times. He said he saw it, but was not convinced that it meant anything.

At this time I was getting angry. I couldn't understand how he could not see the importance of the recording. It was just like the restaurant. There was more to that incident than the news is saying. It's like someone is trying to keep these events quiet.

I stopped rewinding and let the news go on. A news reporter on another station had interview a little boy.

The little boy started to describes the events. He said, "The ceiling opened up and smoke people came and took the kids but I hid under the table. Then the kids came back like magic." His mother grabbed him by his collar and told him to stop telling stories and pulled him away in a hurry. The news reporter laughed and dismissed the child's story as being thought up by an over imaginative kid. Whomever was covering these incidents up didn't do a good job this time. They made two mistakes. One, they didn't clean up the video tape good, and two, they left a witness.

A break, I thought as I looked in amazement. Somebody other than me saw it, and remembered. I needed to talk to that kid and fast. Somebody is covering this thing up. I need to know who and why. Whoever it is has power, and a hell of a lot of it.
I made a few calls to some friends of mine. None of them had clue as to who the little boy was or his mother. Finding the little boy was proving to be too big of a task so I set my sites on other things that I knew I could get done.
I figured I had to get Damon on my side. I thought about showing him the rest of the news but he'd think the kid was just making something up. How could I convince him that something was going on out there? How, how, how?
I called Damon outside on the front porch. The front porch was painted green as it had always been, even when my grandparents were alive. I hadn't got around to doing work on the trees and plants around the exterior of the house. The grass is long and brownish, but overall, the yard looks ok. I sat on the short pillar at the end of the porch. I've always sat there when talking to someone on the porch. I asked Damon to have my back on whatever happens or on

whatever I decide to do because I was going to need him with me. He shook his head but agreed to have my back. I told him to keep his eyes open and question everything that seems out of place. I told him to go home and get some real rest. He asked me if I were going to be alright. I told him we'll be alright here, at least for now.

Damon walked out to his car which was parked in the driveway between the side walk and the street. He got in his car and drove away.

The girls were finished eating their breakfast by now. I went in to see what they were up to. Nalanni was still at the kitchen table watching TV. She had changed the channel to one of her favorite cartoons. When I walked into the kitchen I asked where Paris was. She answered me while never looking at me. She said, "Paris didn't want to watch Sponge Bob, so she went into the living room."

I started to clean off the table when Nalanni asked me, "Why the news people don't tell the truth daddy?"

I asked her, "What do you mean baby?"

She goes on to tell me how, what they said on TV was not the truth and those kids are not real kids any more. I then asked her what she meant by that? She told me, "Because they are not regular kids anymore."

What did Nalanni mean by, "They're not regular kids anymore?" I've seen her do and say some things that can't be ignored, but I never heard her speak the way she's speaking now. What connection does my baby girl have with what's going on? These questions have got to be answered, and soon!

It's 11am and the girls are dressed. I decided to take the girls to eat a light lunch around noon after I run a few errands. The girls seem to not be affected by everything that has happened. They're strong girls like their mother. It's because of them that I'm able to remain strong.

We decided to go get burgers from Quick-n-Split. This place has probably the tastiest burgers in Los Angeles. Their burgers are seasoned just write with a mixture of seasoning salt & pepper. I know the mix well because I had worked there during my college days and again when I was released from jail on probation. My probation officer wanted to make sure I had a job in hopes that I wouldn't go back into my other line of work which landed me in jail in the first place. When we arrived at Quick n Split the crowd was small but growing behind us. There were only two customers before us. When we got to the ordering window I ordered a Super Quick n Split burger with cheese. Paris ordered a cheese burger meal and Nalanni got the scooter wooter meal. We decided to go to Saint Andrews Park to eat our burgers. After we ate our burgers the girls went and played on the swings and jungle gym. Paris pretty much stayed on the swings. Nalanni was all over the place. I stood there with them, and then decided to go have a seat on the closest bench to them. I was about fifteen feet from them so I could easily get to them if I had to. The girls played for about 30 minutes and I thought that it was time to go. The girls had eaten and played.

I gestured to the girls that it was time to go.

Nalanni said, "Can we stay a few more minutes?"

I told her, "Five more minutes and we have to go."

She said, "Ok daddy."

Paris said, "About time. I been ready to go."

Four minutes and a few seconds had passed by when I told Nalanni it was time to go. Nalanni said, she had to use the restroom.

I told Paris to take her. We went to the restrooms on the inside of the gym. The restrooms on the inside were always very clean. The girls went left to the bathrooms and I went right towards the gym.

I could hear laughter, balls bouncing, the sound of little feet slapping the gym floor as small children ran about, and other sounds

from the children playing inside the gym. It must be an open gym day because the summer session was over and the after school program doesn't start until school actually starts. When I got to the doors of the gym I heard a woman's voice from behind me say, "Hey Coach Keith."
I turned around and saw Kendra Johnson. The sound of her voice resonated through my body. Kendra was an old friend. Kendra and I had been on a few dates a couple of years after my wife's death. She liked me and I really liked her but I wasn't ready for a relationship at that time. So we called a time out on each other. Kendra was one of the most beautiful and sexiest women I had ever seen. She was a well put together package. Kendra had beautiful brown skin, she was about 5'6", with a very small waist, nice hips and a perfectly shaped butt. Her butt was the shape of an upside down heart. She use to be the Teen Program counselor and event coordinator here at Saint Andrews Recreation Center. The city thought we were too much like a family here at St. Andrews Park, so they moved people to different parks around the city breaking our little inside the park family apart. Kendra was one of the people they moved. She ended up on the west side somewhere. We fell out of touch after a while.
When I turned around and saw her, I was quickly reminded how beautiful she was.

She ran to me and gave me a huge tight hug as if I was her long lost husband returning to her after being a prisoner of war in Iraq or something. Although I had a puzzled look on my face, it felt damn good to be in her arms. We embraced for what seemed to be two or three minutes but it was more like 20 seconds. As we broke she said, "I was wondering when you were going to come up here. I've been back here for three months now."

"Well, you know I moved away for a while right?"

"No I didn't know that." she said with a surprised look on her face. She then went on to ask me if I had gotten married again.

I quickly told her no. she said, "Oh ok." She looked as if she was relieved that I was still single.

I asked her if she had gotten married. She assured me that she hadn't and was still single. She told me that she used to drive by the house on 83rd street hoping to catch me outside watering the grass or walking to my truck because she didn't have the nerves to walk up to the door. I wish she would have knocked on the door.

I don't know if the expression on my face told it, but I was glad that she was still a single woman.

I heard Nalanni's voice say, "Come on daddy let's go. We finished."

"Is that the baby?" Kendra asked.

"That aint no baby." said Paris.

Kendra turned her head slightly to the right. She saw a preteen aged girl with pretty green eyes. She quickly recognized her. "Wow! You must be Paris."

"Yes, hi Ms. Johnson"

"Oh, you remember me?"

"Yes. You were only the coolest teen counselor here, how could I forget you," Paris said with great enthusiasm.

"They are so big. And they are beautiful too. You're going to need a shotgun and a 9mm."

I say under my breath, *"you have no idea how true that is."*

We talked for a few more minutes. I found myself staring at her. She was still very sexy and her smooth skin still had that golden glow. I was so captivated by her beauty that I could hardly speak. We exchanged phone numbers. I told her that I was living in the house on 83rd street and that I was considering coaching again. I also told her that I would like to see her again. She said she would like that and maybe we could pick up where we left off.

Paris and Nalanni never left my side during my whole conversation with Kendra. They are good girls with a lot of patience. Kendra and I said our goodbyes and hugged one more time. This hug was not as long and intense as the first one, but felt just as good

Chapter 10

While we were hugging, the lights in the gym flickered.

"Wow that has never happened before" said Kendra.

Kendra started walking towards the gym.

The humming started.

"Oh Shit!" I said.

Kendra looked back and said, "Oh shit? Oh shit what?"

She had concern in her voice and sort of puzzled/worried look on her face.

I looked down to make sure the girls were by my side. The girls were starting to look up and I pulled them into the hall way. I instructed them to stay there while I went to go get Kendra, and for them not to look up. I thought Kendra would still be standing by the doors. I peaked in to make sure. She was still there so I reached in, grabbed her by her arm and pulled her out of the gym. She was in a light Trans but quickly snapped out of it. She heard the screams coming from inside the gym. Paris and Nalanni sat down like I told them and didn't move or look towards the gym. Kendra broke free from my grasp and ran towards the gym doors. I stopped her just as she opened the door, but not before she saw them.

Damon was pulling into the parking lot. He got out the car and saw that my truck was parked in the parking lot. A couple of his home boys were standing there against the fence. He gave them a head nod and asked them if they knew where I was. A young man about 20 years old with oversized blue jean shorts, a large white tee shirt and a blue LA Dodgers baseball cap said, "I think he's in the gym."
On the outside things were as normal as they can be. The people in the park went on with their afternoon as normal but on the inside there was total chaos. Kids were been taken and put back in seconds.

Kendra froze as if hit by a stun gun. What she had seen terrified her to the bone. She was so terrified she could not move. A child vanished before her eyes, and mine. I grabbed her and simultaneously put my hand over her mouth to stop the scream she was about to let out.. Only a whimper was allowed to get pass my enormous hands. I drug her away from the gym doors and towards the entrance doors. I told Paris to grab Nalanni and let's go. I looked into the office through the information window and saw Damon looking into the gym through the office observation window. One of the creatures was hovering in front of him but on the other side of the window. Damon could not move. He just stood there, stuck in amazement and fear. We got to the door and Nalanni said, "Wait daddy, I gotta fix um this time." (*In a calm voice.*)

She breaks away from Paris and goes towards the gym doors. I tried to stop her. She turns around looks me in the eyes and says in a calm soft voice, "Daddy it's going to be alright."

Her lips never moved. All at once I was put at ease.

At that moment I knew it would be alright. She had communicated with me on a level that I couldn't explain. The fear of her getting hurt was not in me at the time. I actually wasn't worried at all. She had convinced me that the things inside the gym could do no harm to her, by saying five words, "It's going to be alright." She opens the gym door, and as she did all the beings seemed to be focused on her. The children that disappeared and reappeared were drawn to her as well. She simply touched the wall of the gym and said, "No more." Her voice was calm but demanding.

Damon, still watching through the office observation window could not believe his eyes. He just stood there with his eyes wide open as well as his mouth, saying nothing as the creature that was in front him hovering glided away.

The humming sound stopped, everything seems to go in super slow motion for a few seconds. The beings went back up through their portal. At once all the kids that had been taken suddenly held their heads back and a light shot out of them through their eyes and mouth as if leaving their bodies, then they all collapsed. The movement of the beings and the children never slowed down at all. But everything and everybody else inside the gym did. After all the beings had left and all the children were free of whatever was in them, Nalanni removed her hand from the wall and said, "Ok daddy I'm finish." She took about five steps into the hall, said she was tired, and fell out on the floor, and went to sleep. I thought she collapsed, but she was fast asleep. She was drained. Damon ran over and picked her up. He carried her into the gym office, Paris followed. I ran to make sure my baby girl was ok.

All the children in the gym seemed to be alright. They had no recollection of what had just happened. We went back into the gym to make sure everyone was ok. The children seemed a little tired and disoriented but not hurt. They had all collapsed on the gym floor and had no recollection of the portal opening up or the humming. The adults in the gym thought the lights had only gone out for a few seconds and the kids were just tired from playing. They too were still a little disoriented.

Damon was holding Nalanni and sitting with Paris in the office. Nalanni lay across his lap dead asleep. Paris had not said anything about what has been going on. She didn't seem scared, worried, bothered or excited to any degree. We made our way into the office when Kendra, still a little shaken up grabs me by my arm and says, "Please tell me what just happened here and don't lie to me please." Kendra, usually a strong woman was apparently a bit shaken. Her voice stern but fear was definitely present. She was scared and in disbelief. But would she really believe me if I tell her the truth I thought? She had just seen beings from God know where come through a portal and try to take over children's bodies. The least I could do for her was to tell her the truth.

Damon over heard her and said, "Yes, please tell us what just happened! And what was that thing floating in front of me?"

I told them, "All I know about them is they come in through an opening in the ceilings, like a vortex or something. The openings are a door to an alternate universe or something. The hole or portal is opened when the humming starts."

"You've seen this before?' said Kendra.

"Yes, a couple of nights ago."

"Why you didn't tell me?" said Damon.

"I tried yesterday, Remember? You thought I was tripping. Look, they seem to only want children for some reason." We all looked at each other. Then we looked in the office at Nalanni.

"The girl is the key" Damon remembered. "The man at the gas station told me, "The girl is the key.""

I asked Damon to describe the man. He said the man was tall and about my size. He wore dirty jeans, blue polo type shirt, and a long dirty tan rain coat. It's August. Why would you need an overcoat in August? It's been about 80 degrees outside all week.

Damon had just described the man that was at the hospital the night Nalanni was born, and I think the same man was watching the girls and I leave the restaurant. I needed to talk to him. We exited the gym once we knew everyone was alright. Just like before at the restaurant, the people outside were oblivious to the events inside. They were calling this a 2 minute blackout. Kendra, the girls, and I got to my truck. Damon got in his car and we drove back to the house.

So far all of the events had taken place inside. Maybe these things need a solid, enclosed surface to come through. Why are they after the kids? They take them briefly then return them without anybody realizing that they were gone. What are they doing with the kids in such a short time?

These are the questions that pondered my mind over and over.

We arrived at the house on 83rd around
1:45pm. Damon had gotten there before us.
He was sitting on the porch quiet as if
locked in a Trans or something. I opened the
door to let the girls and Kendra in. Nalanni
was still asleep so I carried her in and laid
her on the couch. I went back out on the
porch to talk to Damon. He just stared at the
street only turning his head to view people
walking down the street or cars driving by. I
asked him what was up with him and what
was on his mind? He looked at me in a
scared and humbling way. Shaking his head
he said, "These people don't even have a
clue. I mean know body has the slightest
idea what's happening or why. Not even us
bro."
"I know what you mean. I've been dealing
with this for a couple of days now. How do
you think I felt? I thought I was losing my
mind or in some horrific, bad ass dreaming."
Damon turns and looks at a neighbor
washing his car. He starts to shake his head
again wondering, what is all of this about?
Why the kids?
I tell him, "I don't know yet. All I know is; I
have two daughters that I need to take care
of, one who seems to have some special
effect on these things and the other who
doesn't seemed worried one bit about what's
going on.
Damon said, "Yeah, what's up with that

bro? How did Nalanni do that shit?"

"Man Damon, I don't know. All I know is that, she started showing signs that she could do incredible stuff around three years ago and I dismissed them as coincident.
I had seen this whole ordeal unfold right before my eyes and I still couldn't believe it."

Damon turns to me and says, "It don't matter if we believe it or not. This shit is happening, here and now!"

We both sat there realizing that all the Boogie Man stories and other things that go bump in the night could actually be true.

Chapter 11

I walked into the house thinking about the conversation Damon and I had just had. He was right. This shit is really happening. But, how far are these events taking place? Are they just happening here in Los Angeles, all over California, or all over the world?
My only concern at the moment was to make sure my girls were safe here in Los Angeles, Ca. This weird, sci-fi shit was happening right here, right now! I thought, "This kind of shit only happens on TV to white people. But here we are here in South Central Los Angeles.
I went into the house and took a seat at the kitchen table. I was starting to question my sanity. I've questioned many things in my life. Evolution, The Holy Bible, if psychics are real, Area 51, politicians, even if we were actually alone in the universe, but never my sanity.

I sat there for several minutes, and as I sat there pondering I couldn't help but think about my daughters. Nalanni was sleep, Paris and Kendra sat with her in the living room. Where and how did Nalanni get the abilities to do the things she can do? And why is Paris so calm about these ordeals? There are a lot of questions that need to be answered.

I stepped into the foyer and looked at Nalanni sleeping on the couch. Kendra had been sitting next to her the whole time. She had been watching me while I was looking at Nalanni. Paris looked up at me from the floor but quickly returned her focus back to the TV. Paris didn't seem the least bit worried about her younger sister.

Then out of nowhere Paris says, "Don't worry about her dad. She's straight."

I look at Paris and say, "What, what are you talking about, she's straight?"

"Yeah that's right. She's straight," said Paris.

"And how do you know that young lady?"

"She told me she was tired and needed to get some rest before the next time came."

"Next time? What next time? Talk to me Paris. What next time?"

"I don't know dad. That's all she told me."

"I didn't hear her say anything."

"That's because she speaks to me in my head."

"She does what?"

"She stalks to me without talking. I can hear

her in my mind."

"Hold up. Hold up. Are you telling me that she can communicate with you telepathically?"

"If that's what it means, then yes."

"How long has she been doing that?"

"She started in the restaurant. She told me what was about to happen and not to stare at the ceiling. She also told me that they can't hurt me because she was in me."

"She was in you? What does that mean?"

Damon walked in just as Paris begins to tell how it happened but he just stood there not saying a word.

"Well, remember the time when we were playing in the backyard and Nalanni cut her finger? I saw her do it. It looked like she did it on purpose but I wasn't sure. She started crying and I ran over to her. She was bleeding on the tip of her index finger. She was like freaking out because of the blood. Without thinking I stuck her finger in my mouth and sucked the blood off and spit it out. I then stuck my finger with a nail and told her if we rub our fingers together on the cuts it'll stop hurting. We rubbed our bloody fingers together and she said now I was in her and she was in me."

"But why doesn't she communicate with me like that?"

"She said that she did but you weren't ready to except it."

"What the hell does she mean I'm not

ready?"

All at once everybody looked at me as if saying, look how you are acting right now. I stood there for a minute, realized I was acting erratically and said, "Ok, ok I get it."

After realizing that my youngest daughter actually knew me very well, I couldn't help to think, where and how she got these special abilities. I thought and thought and thought, but I couldn't pin point where the powers had come from. It was starting to feel like I was dreaming again. I cupped my face into my hands and when I removed them Nalanni was standing in front of me.

"Are you alright daddy," She asked?

I grabbed her and gave a big hug.

"I'm good baby," I said to her."

She then said, "Don't worry daddy we'll be alright."

"Mom told me to be strong for you and Paris."

"But you never met your mom."

"Yes I did. She used to talk to me while I was inside of her stomach. She told me I would be able to do things that people wouldn't understand. And that I shouldn't tell people about these things."

The whole time she was talking to me, she

never moved her lips and kept her eyes on mine. But I heard her loud and clear. She had been communicating with me the whole time telepathically. She was letting me know that I am ready to receive her thoughts as words to me. I just sat and stared at her.

Chapter 12

I sat in the room about half an hour before
Kendra had walked in. She walked in and
sat next to me on my queen size bed. The
room was mildly lit. It was the first time any
woman besides my wife had ever sat on the
bed. Kendra wasn't just any woman. She
was the first and last woman I dated that I
really liked. It seemed as if she got me just
like Nakol did.
When she sat on the bed, she looked at me
and said, "All this stuff is really happening.
It's like, someone should come on a loud
speaker and say we have just arrived in the
twilight zone in a Rod Sterling voice."
But there was no Rod Sterling voice or any
other voice of reason.
I said, "No baby, this is for real."
She looked at me with this look of great
hope and despairs at the same time and said,
"I want to be with you through it all and

where ever it takes us."

She then leaned in close to me and we kissed. I quickly remembered what it was like to kiss her sweet thick lips. Her lips had always been soft and moist. I remember the sweet taste of her lips and tongue as they gently touch my lips and tongue. Her breath was always fresh. I pulled her close to me. She gave no resistance to the idea of being close to me. I wanted her and she wanted me.

A voice coming from the direction of the bedroom door said, "Daddy." We quickly separated as if we were high school kids being walked in on by one of our parents.

It was Paris. She had come in to ask me what was for dinner. I told her I would be in there in a minute. She said ok and went back down the hall.

Kendra asked if I wanted her to make dinner. I told her no and that I would do it. She then said, "Relax and let a woman cook you a meal for a change."

She was a good cook. I remember staying at her house on occasion and she would cook these delicious meals for us. Her fried chicken was to die for. Thinking about her cooking got me hungry and curious about what she had in mind for dinner.

She prepared some country fried chicken breast, macaroni and cheese, French cut green beans, and dinner rolls. For desert we had strawberry sundaes with nuts on top, and of course whipped cream.

We sat down to eat dinner around 7:45pm. Damon even stayed for dinner. Everybody was looking for a good home cooked meal that I didn't cook. Although I was a good cook, they wanted that woman's touch on a meal. There was very little conversation at the dinner table. I guess everyone was so into the meal that they had no time for talking.

After dinner I signaled for the girls to head to the bathroom for their baths before bed. As always they took their baths together. I liked it this way so Paris could make sure Nalanni bathed correctly. Although she had all these special abilities, she was still a five year old when it came to things like bathing, brushing her teeth, folding her clothes, and stuff like that. The girls bathed for about 15 minutes and I walked down the hall and tapped on the door and told them it was time to get out the tub. They stayed in the bathroom for another 10 - 15 minutes before coming out fully dressed in their sleeping clothes. I tucked in Paris first. I kissed her on the forehead and said good night. Nalanni was watching as I tucked her older sister in. She looked at me with concern as if she was worried about me. As I walked over to her she cracked a smile as if she was glad it was her turn to be tucked in. I told her that I was ready for everything to come. She said, "I know you are daddy."

I gave her a kiss on her cheek and said good night to her. Got up off my knees and told the girls that I would see them in the morning. I kept the night light on that sat on top of the dresser so the room would not be totally dark. I turned back to look at them once more before I left the room. I left the door slightly open as a sense of safety for the girls. It at least made me feel a little better to know that they were comfortable in their room. I left the door open so that I may here if something were to happen in their room.

Chapter 13

The children's home on west Adams
Boulevard was calm and quiet. The now
quiet building had given way to screaming,
active children all day long. It was now bed
time and the last of the crack babies were
being put to rest by the charming head nurse
and home mother Ms. Marx. Ms. Marx had
been the house mother of the Adams house
for over twenty years. Ms. Marx didn't have
any biological children of her own but loved
children all the same. She had taken in her
niece and nephew when she was twenty
seven years old. Her sister had both children
out of wedlock. She had been too busy
running the streets, using drugs, and chasing
after her dope dealer boyfriends. She chose

theses type of men because of their access to drugs, in particular, cocaine in forms, powder or crack. Sharon had been on drugs since she was a teenage kid. The oldest child was a boy. He was 3years old at the time and the other was a girl. She was only two weeks old. Both children were born with cocaine in their systems. The doctors and staff are required to inform Children Services by law when a child is born with narcotics in their systems.

Ms. Marx was their only known relative. She gladly took them in and raised them as her own children. Every since then she had been taking in as many as twenty children at a time. She has always had a large heart and a large house to go with it. Her house sat on the corner of Adams and Victoria. The house is a six large bedroom house with a large kitchen and dining room, three and a half bath rooms, game/TV room, with a large backyard. The house was originally a large 3 bedroom home. She added the three extra rooms for more children. The government had given her the money for the expansion of the house for the purpose of caring for children that were taken by the courts from parents that had drug or alcohol addictions. Although the government paid her very well, she really did this out of the kindness of her heart. She genuinely cared for these children. All of them.

Ms. Marx sat in the living room area rocking a four month old baby girl that wouldn't go to sleep. The baby had been born prematurely. Her mother did heroin until she went into labor. The living room was dark and cool on this warm summer night. She had been rocking the young child for about 15 minutes and the baby was just starting to fall asleep. Her eyes were closing and she was totally relaxed.

Suddenly the house began to shake. The children that were not awake woke up abruptly and ran down stairs to where Ms. Marx was rocking the baby to sleep. The ones that were still asleep also woke up and ran down stairs. Once all the children were all in the same room, the humming started. Kids were screaming in all different tones because of the different ages and genders. At once all of the screaming stopped. The humming got louder. Now all eyes were on the ceiling. Kids started vanishing and reappearing all over the room. Ms. Marx never looked up, but glanced at the children to see why there was no screaming. She saw Andrew, a seven year old boy disappear and reappear right before her eyes, then another, and another, and another. That's when she peeked up and saw them; The Ebulliti. The ghostly, gas like beings. She stared at them for a few seconds then quickly closed her eyes. Her fear wouldn't allow her to take another peek. She was literally frozen still with fear. After about two minutes the humming stopped and all the kids were getting up off the floor. Ms. Marx eyes opened and she got up and checked on the kids. She asked if everyone was alright. All at once they answered, "Yes, we are fine," and they all quietly went back to their rooms. Ms. Marx was bewildered by the way they all answered at once and went to bed without one single child fussing. This was like an earth moving event and no fuss. Not one single child fussed or complained. These were kids that were born with drug habits of all kinds. Most of them have to be medicated to go sleep, and during the day so they can behave close to normal. They are never quiet, even when they are sleep. She starts to think. What happened to them? What did those things do to them? Ms. Marx being the concerned and caring house mother she was, decided to go upstairs to check on the children. She went to each room and to her surprise all the children were sound asleep. As she goes from room to room she couldn't stop visualizing the kids disappearing and reappearing. The strange thing about all the kids was the fact that they were all sleeping on their backs with their arms lying straight by their sides.

"That's odd," she thought as she continued to check each room.

Chapter 14

There was a knock at the door. Ms. Marx
was startled by the loud knocks on the door.
She was wondering who could be at the door
at this hour. Again four more loud knocks at
the door (*knock, knock, knock, knock)!* Ms.
Marx still shaken from the previous events
asked in an unsure voice, "Who's there?"
There was no answer. She asked again,
"Who's there?" She starts to get nervous and
worried. This was no ordinary evening for
Ms. Marx and her crew. There were a total
of five crew members that helped Ms. Marx
throughout the day. Two during the late
night to early morning and two throughout
the day. The other was one of the two first
kids she had taken in, Shelli her niece. Shelli
lived in the house and helped out during the
changing of shifts and overnight. Shelli was
a fair skinned, thin, and very smart young
lady.
Shelli had heard the knocks and was curious
as well. No one ever comes there at this hour
unless it was an emergency, and even then

they would call and announce their arrival and purpose. No one had called all night. The knocks sounded off again. *knock, knock, knock, knock!* This time even louder than before. Ms. Marx shouted, "Who's there!" Still there was no answer. Now more scared than nervous, she looks up stairs to where Shelli was standing. Shelli looks at her and says, "Don't answer it!" The house was still kind of dark inside but there was enough light to see around the room. Ms. Marx slowly starts to make her way towards the door. It was11pm and she was wondering who could it be. As she steps into the foyer, a voice says, "Is everything alright in there Ms. Marx? It's LAPD. Ms. Marx feeling relieved hurries to the door and opens it. "Is everything alright ma'am?"

"No! They came out the hole in the ceiling. There was a loud humming sound. All the kids disappeared then reappeared. The things, I saw them! I saw them!" Ms. Marx was hysterical and not making sense at all.

The police officer had come with two other officers. The other two officers had not said a word. The officer asks her to calm down, but she was too pumped up at the moment. One of the other officers pulled out a device which looked like a cell phone, but the screen was lit up like a red stop light. One of the other police officers said, "It has begun. We are too late." The other officer pulls out a silver ball from a pouch he had thrown over his shoulder. It was about the size of a golf ball. He gives it a twist and places it on the coffee table. The silver ball starts to spin counter clockwise. It spins faster and faster. Ms. Marx and Shelli are so captivated by the silver spinning ball that they don't see the officers leave. The officers had backed out of the house so smoothly and quickly that they weren't noticed leaving. Ms. Marx slowly started walking over to the silver spinning ball. Looking at it curiously and closely. The ball then started glowing a bright gold color. It got so bright that they could no longer look at it, and then BOOM! It exploded with enough force to level the house completely, and seriously damage the houses next door on both sides. Who were those men? What had they been too late for and what had already begun? They destroyed the house and everything in it. No survivors!

Chapter 15

Nalanni woke up screaming, "NO! Daddy
no!"
Kendra and I were lying on the couch
watching TV. We heard the screaming. I
jumped up and ran down the hall to the
girl's room. Kendra followed. Paris was
sitting up staring at Nalanni. Nalanni was
sitting up shaking profusely. While sobbing
she started saying, "Daddy I couldn't save
um." Tears were streaming down her face.
She said it several times before she stopped
crying and went back to sleep.
Kendra was talking to Paris, trying to get her
to relax and go back to sleep. I was holding
Nalanni in my arms. Damon was at the bed
room door looking in. He had come down
the hall from the kitchen right behind us. He
had his gun in his hand but held at his side
and out of the girl's site. He always carried
his gun. He had a motto. *"I would rather be*

judged by twelve than carried by six." Once we got the girls to calm down we went back into the kitchen.

The TV was on. A breaking news bulletin came on. There were firemen putting out a fire. A large two story house seemed to be burning.

The volume was low so I asked Damon to turn it up. A reporter was reporting that a house exploded on West Adams Blvd. around 10:55pm. Everybody in the house had died in the explosion. She reported that approximately 25 - 30 children were inside along with 2 - 3 adults. They flashed a picture of Ms. Marx on the TV. The house was reported to be the Adams House. A home for kids that had been taken away from their parent's because of substance abuse.

We heard a voice. We turned around and it was Nalanni standing at the kitchen door. "Daddy I couldn't help them. I couldn't help them. I couldn't help them! She was crying and repeating *"I couldn't help them!"*

I thought, how could she have helped them, unless they were victims of the Ebulliti?

The news stated that the cause of the explosion had not been determined yet. Faulty wiring and a gas leak were the suspected reasons. There hadn't been any fatalities in any of the other events. If this event was connected to the others, why fatalities now?

What made this event any different from all the others? Could this have really been an accident and mere coincidence? The one thing that's for sure is, I needed to find out. And I needed to find out fast.

Kendra got up to tend to Nalanni and put her back to bed. She turned and gave me a look like, let me handle this. I remained seated for a few seconds as I watched them walk through the dining room and turn down the hall. As they turned the corner my attention went back to the news. They were playing it safe as to not give up too much information. While they were interviewing the Fire Chief, Damon said, "Hold up! Rewind that, stop right there. Play that part. I pressed play on the DVR. Damon instructed me to pause it. Pointing at a man standing behind the Fire chief; he said, "That's that fool I saw at the gas station.

I said, "Are you sure?"

"Hell yeah I'm sure!"

I got closer to the TV. The man he was referring to looked familiar to me also but, I couldn't put my finger on it at the time.

Damon said it was the same man that was talking to him at the gas station but he was cleaner. What was this mystery man's connection to what was going on? I stared at the image for at least two minutes. Then it hit me. This was the same man I saw outside of the restaurant in the parking lot and the man that had held a conversation with me the night my wife died and Nalanni was born.

"Shit Damon, I saw this man outside the restaurant. This man was at the hospital the night Nakol died and Nalanni was born. I started checking my memory bank for his name. I whispered to myself, "What was his name?"

I was surprised that I could not remember his name. I am usually good with names. I went back to that night in my mind. I spent years trying not to think about that night and the devastation is caused us. But recent events have put me in and urgency to relive those unforgotten but never thought about moments of despair. I had to relive the doctor telling me that one, and only one of them was going live. The feeling I felt as I watched my wife's life slowly leaving her body as I was forced out of the room feeling helpless. My wife and child were fighting for their lives. A fight in which only one of them would come out alive. Then this asshole named James Harris tells me everything is going to be alright. That's it! James Harris is his name. I had remembered his name. James Harris had been the man at the hospital, restaurant, gas station with my brother, and now at the scene of a huge fatal disaster. Who are you James Harris? I asked myself over and over again while sitting at the kitchen table. I burned that name and face into my brain.

Damon said, "We need to find this mutha fucka bro!"

I agreed with him. But how do we find him? If we drove to the scene of the accident, will he still be there?

I couldn't leave Kendra and the girls alone on a maybe. Other than the hospital, he has never tried to contact me in any way. He even expressed genuine concern for Nalanni at the hospital. With all this in mind I asked Damon what exactly did he say to him at the gas station.

Damon said, "He told me to go to the house on 83rd because you were going to need me and that the girl is the key. I asked him what girl but he never said who the girl was. When I got in my car I looked up and he was gone."

"Is that all he said to you?"

"Basically that's all he said."

"Are you positive?"

"Man check this out. He was talking to me like he knew me. He said my name and yours."

"Did he get loud or aggressive?"

"That's the strange thing, he was calm. He was calm even when I pulled out my heat."

Damon and I discussed the James Harris connection to all this for about thirty more minutes. It's well after midnight now and I was getting tired. I didn't want to go to sleep but I knew I needed to be rested at all times just in case. James Harris and his connection to all that has happened is constantly burning in my head. I wanted it to keep burning there until I got to the bottom of this.

Chapter 16

It's 6am and the girls are already up watching cartoons. Kendra was awake also. She had remained in the bed watching the news. They were still reporting on last night's accident. I was aware but not fully awake yet. I didn't go to sleep until about 2am. Kendra had gone to bed right after putting Nalanni back to bed. Paris had slept through the night after Nalanni had awakened screaming. Paris is a strong worry free kid that gets good grades and is in good physical shape. She's actually kind of tough to be so pretty. She looks so much like her mother.

I rolled over in the bed. I was facing Kendra but my eyes were not open. I felt her nudge me. She nudged me again then said my name. "Keith."

She nudged me one more time and I opened my eyes. She then asked me who James Harris was. I replied, "Who?"

She said, "James Harris. You kept saying that name in your sleep."

I knew James Harris was on my mind but I could not believe I said his name in my sleep. I told her that he's a man that keeps popping up at most of the events. She quickly asked me if he had been at the park the day before. I said, "If he was I didn't see him." That was a good question. Why wasn't he at the park? Or maybe he was but we just didn't see him. There was no way to tell for sure, so I dismissed that idea and moved on. We lay in the bed for about an hour or so then the girls came in and asked what's for breakfast. I asked them what they wanted. They answered at the same time but gave two different answers. Paris wanted me to make my famous instant oatmeal and Nalanni wanted cereal. I just let them know they both could have what they wanted. I got up to make their breakfast. Paris attended to Nalanni while I made her oatmeal. The oatmeal was easy to make. I just added a little sugar, butter, cinnamon, and a dash of coffee creamer. It was simple

but the girls loved it. I made myself and
Kendra some bacon. Damon and the girls
smelled the bacon and decided they wanted
some also. I made the first slices for the girls
then I made some for Kendra, Damon, and I.
Everybody sat down and ate their meals. I
asked Nalanni if she remembered last night.
She told me she did but everything is ok
now. I asked her if she wanted to talk about
it and she told me no. I told her that I needed
to ask her one more question. I looked her in
her eyes and asked her if she knew James
Harris. To my surprise she said, "Yes.
That's the name he goes by for now. I can't
tell you his real name yet."
I asked her, "Why not?"
"Because it's not time yet."
"Well, what does he want?"
"Dad you said you only had one more
question?"
"Ok, ok, just tell me what he wants."
She said, "He's my guardian. He helps keep
me safe."
She looked at me and said, "Can I go watch
Sponge Bob now?"
I had to catch myself. I was losing sight of
the fact that Nalanni is still just a five year
old child. She's my daughter and I can't and
won't forget that.

She said he is her guardian and that he
watches over her and protects her. Part of
me was mad because she accepted the idea

of him being her guardian. I mean, what have I been doing all her life? My conscious kicked me in the head and put my ego back in check. I needed to stay focused on the real issues here and not any ego driven scenarios. Focus, focus, focus, I thought as I reentered the name James Harris into my mind.

Who is James Harris? This is the million dollar question. Thoughts of who or what he could actually be danced around my head like juiced up break dancers. I thought, "Is he even human?" What planet is he from? How can I find him? Is he alone or are there others like him? These questions were going through my head over and over again. I had been sitting there thinking about these questions for so long that I lost track of time. When I finally stopped thinking about James Harris I looked around and I was the only one left in the kitchen. I had been sitting there for about half an hour. Damon was gone and Kendra was in the back of the house helping the girls get dressed. No matter what, I knew I needed to find out who, what, where, why and how James Harris is connected to all of this.

Chapter 17

Damon had left the house on 83rd street to go home to get a fresh change of clothes. He had been at my house for a couple of days now. He could have just showered at my house, but his need to go home and be alone to collect his thoughts pulled him back to his home on 90th street. He had no clothes at my house and my clothes would not fit him.

He was bigger than me in width but I am several inches taller.

Damon left driving down 83rd east towards Normandie. A gray Chevy Impala with dark tinted windows was parked on 83rd on the other side of Western Avenue. He could see that there was someone sitting in the car so he slowed down to try and get a peek inside. He couldn't see inside the car clearly, because the windows were too dark. He drove pass the car heading east. When Damon got half way down the block the car pulled away from the curb and started heading in the same direction he was going. Damon noticed the car but thought they might just be undercover police officers. He had his gun on his lap at the time but quickly put it in his stash spot. He had a stash spot built into his car for moments like this. This spot was undetected by police during a routine search but could be found when an extensive search was being performed.

Damon knew his license, registration, and insurance were up to date. He also knew he couldn't lead the police to his house, so instead of turning right towards his house, he turned left on Normandie going north. He thought he would try and lose them but without committing any traffic violations.

He headed north down Normandie. He crossed Florence Blvd heading towards Gage. The car was still following him. He was starting to wonder why they don't just pull him over. He made a left on 65th street heading west. The car and whoever was inside was still on his tail. Damon kept going west down 65th street until he got to Denker Ave. There was now light at Denker, just a stop sign. He decided he would try to be a little slick now. He pulled up to the stop sign slowly. He watched as the cars went by him in both directions. He knew he had to time the cars just right. He knew if he pulled this off he would have a little breathing room between him and the person or persons in the Impala. A light green Volkswagen Bug passed by going north and a black Maxima passed by going south and a red Honda was approaching from the south with a long line of vehicles behind it. The same amount of traffic was approaching from the north. This was his chance. He knew if he jumped out behind the Maxima but before the Honda, the car following him would be stuck in the approaching traffic. As soon as the Maxima passed he punched the gas just enough to fall in behind the Maxima without causing the Honda to slow down. Now there were several cars passing. Most important, the Impala couldn't follow him. He looked in his rear view mirror and said, "That's right motha fuckas, I got skills!" Damon had gotten away from whoever was following him, or so he thought. He headed south down Denker. He didn't speed or anything, he just at a good safe speed to be able to see the Chevy approaching from the rear. He pulled up to the house. Everything seemed normal on his block. There were kids playing outside. He didn't notice any strange vehicles parked on the block. He wanted to make sure the persons in the gray car or anyone else hadn't followed him. No one had followed him. To make sure he parked behind the apartments next door to his house. He sat there to see if any cars would come speeding back to where he was. Or if anyone came back there with guns drawn screaming police! No cars had come, nor did anyone come screaming police. He got out of the car and walked over to a cinder block wall that separated the apartment's property from his. He stood on a crate and peeked over the wall to view his driveway, backdoor, garage, and part of his backyard. Everything looked to be in order. He took one more look around to see if anyone was watching him. He saw no one. He quickly pulled himself to the top of the wall, looked down his driveway toward the street, then right towards his garage, put his feet on the top of the wall, swung them over and jumped down. There was a clean straight line of about 22 feet from the wall to his back door. He focused on the black, iron and metal, mesh bar door. He had clamped his keys to his belt loop when he got out of his BMW. Clamping his keys to his belt loop with a metal clamp was a habit he picked up from me.

Damon quickly ran over to the bar door, unhooked his keys, quickly found the key that opened the door, put the key in the lock, turn the key then paused as if he forgot something or as if someone said wait. No one had said wait. There are two locks on his back door, a door knob and a deadbolt lock. He knew he always locked them both when he left the house. He usually unlocks the dead bolt then the knob lock. When he turned the dead bolt the door had slightly opened. That only happens when the bottom lock is not locked, he thought in his mind. He reached down to get his gun but it was not in his waist. He didn't take out of the stash when he got out of the car. He knows there is a gun in a basket under some dirty clothes just four feet from the door and several other guns throughout the house, but those didn't matter at the time. The one in the basket was the only one that matter now. He wondered if someone had been in his house, and are they still inside? He looked down at the locks and around the door to see if he can see any signs that the locks have tampered with. He sees no evidence of tampering. He thought about going back to his car to get his gun, then thinks about the gun just four feet away. He knew if someone was inside, they would have the drop on him, and having a gun wouldn't really matter. He pulled his key out of the lock and slowly backed away from the door. He decided he would go back over the wall to get his gun from his car. He backed up all the way to the wall, not taking his eyes off the back door of his house. When he got to the wall he looked for something to stand on so he could climb over the wall quicker and easier. He's not as tall as I am, so going over the wall will be a task without some leverage to make it quick and easy. The wall is at least 6 feet tall and he is only 5'10". He turns and sees a bucket next to the garage. He quickly gets it and puts it next to the wall, stands on it and thrust himself up and over the wall. He runs over to his BMW unlocks the door with his remote. He has to stick the key into his ignition and turn on the power in the car so he can activate the stash box. The stash box opens, he grabs his gun, turns the car power off, closes his door quietly, and goes back over to the six foot wall. He stands on the crate and slowly peeks over the wall to see if anything has changed during the short trip to his car. Although every thing looked to be in order, he knew it wasn't. Someone had been in or is still in his house. He jumps and pulls himself to the top of the wall. This time he turns and sits on the wall and swings his legs and feet around to face his house. He leaps down landing on his feet. He stays in a crouching position for a few seconds. It was an attempt to stay low and out of sight. He pulls his gun from his waist and holds it by his side. He creeps quickly towards the door in a slight crouch like position. He made sure to leave the door unlocked so he could easily and quietly enter. The door was still unlocked. He grabbed the knob and turned it. It didn't make a sound. He slowly pushed the door open and peeked in. He could partially see into the kitchen which was to the left. The stove, kitchen counter and sink were visible from the back door. As he opened the door a little more, the basket with the clothes and gun became visible. It didn't appear to be moved in any way. He stepped his left foot up and into the threshold of the door while pushing the door open with his left hand. He kept his left foot against or close to the door just in case someone was behind the door and tried to push door against his head or to make him drop the gun. The door would hit his foot first. And would not cause much impact if any. He pushes the open wide enough for him to get in. Now the whole laundry room was visible to him. But still only part of the kitchen was exposed to his line of sight. He steps the other foot in and peeks around the corner to his left and the rest of the kitchen was visible and empty. The kitchen cabinets were closed and hadn't appeared to open. Whoever was in the house did not ransack the kitchen.

There were two entrance ways into the kitchen. One to the dining room which was straight in front of him and the other to the hallway which was on his left. He decided to go towards the hallway. He had to walk around a small table of about four feet in width. He stayed close to the table, switching the gun direction back and forth from entrance to entrance. He reached the entrance to the hall. His heart was pounding in his chest. He peeked around the corner to his left then to his right. Straight across the hall from the kitchen was a bathroom, and to his left was a room he used for storage. The bathroom door was open. It was a small bathroom that was pretty much totally visible through the door. He didn't feel the bathroom held a threat so he went to the room he used for storage. The door was closed. He knew the only things that should be in that room was a bed and some boxes. He opened the door and pushed it all the way open. He could see the whole inside of the room except the closet. He slowly went in. It was dusty from the lack of use. The bed was covered with medium size boxes. Large boxes were stacked up at least five feet at the foot of the bed. The room was fairly dusty but organized. He slowly made his way to the closet door. The closet was no

more than four feet from him. He
approached it slowly and quietly. He all of a
sudden became more conscious of the
sounds he might make with each step. He
got within two feet of the door. He looked
down at the knob hesitating to open it. He
knew the closet was small but big enough
for a person or two to hide inside it. His
heart rate increased as he reached down to
grab the door knob. He took a deep breath,
grabbed the knob and turned. The door
easily came open. No one was inside.
Besides the bed and boxes, the room was
empty. He left that room and slowly went to
the next bedroom which was on the other
side of the bathroom. Was Damon being
paranoid because of the events that have
transpired over the last couple of days or
was his paranoia warranted? Why would
someone want to be in his house in broad
daylight? Jackers would wait until it's dark
so they won't be seen. Thieves wouldn't
bother locking the door once they were in,
and besides that, the house was still neat.
Maybe whoever was in there had already
left and Damon had missed them. Or maybe
he never locked the other lock in the first
place.
He got to the other bedroom and the door
was already open. Damon never closes that
door. He took a deep breath and let out a
sigh. He thinks this is the room he should
have check first because this where his safe

is. From the door he could see that the room was empty. He turns to the closet and slowly approaches it. The intruders could not be in this closet or at least he hope there was no one in there. Damon walks over to the closet door. His bathrobe still hangs on the door along with a few shirts. His cash from his street activities was stored in a floor safe in the closet. Maybe the intruders were there to rob him. This closet was just as small as the other. If there were intruders, only one would be able to fit inside the closet. The closet door was slightly crack which made his already bumping heart skip a beat or two. Without hesitation he reaches down and snatches the door open. The closet was empty of any persons. They was still covered by a small piece of carpet the concealed the small safe. After opening the safe and finding that the contents were still inside. Damon really starts to question the motives of his home's possible intruder/s. He gets caught up in thought and sits on the edge of his bed. He catches himself and jumps up to continue checking his house for the intruders.

He moves slowly down the hall towards the front of the house. He carefully and methodically takes each step with caution. He knows there are spots in the hall that creek and crack when stepped on. He also knows where those spots are. He continues down the hall avoiding those noise making spots. He approaches the door with his left shoulder against the wall and looks inside with his gun drawn and extended out about two feet from his body at chest level. Nothing looked to be out of place so far and he had already checked 4 rooms in the house including the kitchen. Since the living room and dining room are connected there was one more room to check. He came out of the bedroom and looked down the hall to his right toward the rooms he had already checked. All was clear. Then he looked back to his left heading toward the living room. He was about five steps from the living room but it seemed more like thirty feet because of the anxiety he was experiencing. He was nervous and sweating. The house was extremely quiet. The only sound being made was the sound from the refrigerator motor which hummed smooth and semi quietly. He could still here the house cracking as he took each step. The house was built in the early 30's so it made sounds as you moved through it. He kept his left shoulder on the wall as he nervously approached the living room. His heart was pumping hard like a base drum in his chest. He wondered what or who was waiting for him in the last room of the house. He thought about yelling out, "Who's in here? Is anybody there?" But, he decided to stay in stealth mode. As he got to the end of the wall he could see the whole dining room to his right. In his view was his marble top dining table, a china cabinet that was left to him by our mother. He turned his body to the right which put his back against the wall. To his left and around the corner was the living room. Facing the dining room with his back against the wall, he took in a deep breath, and when he exhaled, he flung around the corner with his gun held out and high. He felt as if he was in a movie and moving in slow motion but there wasn't any music, no lights, no camera, just slow motion action. When he stopped, there was no one there. His 50 inch T.V. hang on the wall about 24 feet in front of him. His black, leather furniture suggested that he was a bachelor. Other than a few Sports Illustrated Magazines that lay on the table, the living room was spotless. He took in another deep breath but let it out as a sigh of relief. His heart was still pumping fast and hard. He just shook his head and said to himself, "I'm tripping. I must have left one of the locks unlocked. Man I'm slippin and trippin." He put his gun back in his waist and walked to the window near the front door. There were off white vertical blinds hanging in the window. Damon pulled the one closest to the door to the side so he could look out. He had to check and see if there were any strange vehicles parked on the block or driving by. For the moment everything looked clear. He was calming down now but felt as if he was being watched. His heart was beating almost normal now and his breathing had calmed also. He wondered who had been following him earlier and were they still watching him now? Were they targeting him or anyone that left the house on 83rd St. I need to call my brother, he thought. He pulled out his cell phone and called me. He explained the whole scene to me from the moment he noticed the car sitting on the other side of Western Avenue, to the chase and how he eluded them. I told him to make sure there is no one around watching him, to stay safe, and get back here to my house as soon as possible. Instead of showering there he decided to come back to my house to shower. He went to his room, packed up some clothes and more of his guns and proceeded to leave out the back door.

Chapter 18

James Harris had watch Damon the whole time since he entered his home on west 90th street. He carefully watched as Damon went through his house nervously. James Harris had been careful not to be seen by him. What Damon didn't know was that, James Harris had already been in his house and place surveillance devices throughout the house. The devices transmitted directly to Harris' mind instead of to a monitoring device. Harris' technology was extremely advanced. He knew he had to make contact with them, but the time had to be right. He also knew that Nalanni was going to need his protection for a little while longer, until she was strong enough to at least protect herself from the Ebulliti. She was still quite young. Although her instincts are sharp, she needs more time to tune into all of her powers. James Harris knew this world couldn't afford for her to fail. This whole world is riding on this little girl's development. SHE CANNOT FAIL!

Damon finished packing up his things and proceeded to leave his house. He decided he would leave the way he came. He checked all the windows in the house to make sure they were locked and went out the back door. He made sure all the door locks were locked as well. Of all the checking he did, he didn't see the surveillance devices that had placed in the house because they were biomechanical. They have the ability to camouflage with the surface they are attached to and move around and reposition themselves. He went out the back door and straight to the brick wall. He stood on top the crate and dropped his bag on the other side of the wall. The bag was strong. It's one of the bags he had gotten from his brother. I used these types of duffle bags to hold the basketball equipment for my teams. Damon got to the top of the fence and jumped down. He grabbed the duffle bag and headed towards his car. He pulled his keys and pushed the button to open the trunk. He through the bag in the trunk but made sure he kept a gun with him inside the car. He turned the car around so he could be driving forward out of the driveway in case he needed to make some quick driving moves.

He slowly crept down the driveway. His senses were on full alert hoping to see his pursuers in time to get away if he had to. When he got to the street he saw nothing out of the ordinary. He went towards Budlong avenue taking his might be pursuers away from the direction he needed to go. He made sure no one was following him and made his way to the house on 83rd street.

Damon arrived back at the house without incident. No one had followed him and there were no strange cars parked on the block or at least none in plain sight.

James Harris needs to make contact with Nalanni and her family without causing alarm. He needed to find a way to make them trust him. He knows Nalanni is not strong enough to beat the Ebulliti. His world had fallen to the Ebulliti, and earth was the only place his people could flourish without conflict. Besides, they had discovered the earth before the Ebulliti. He had spent his whole time on earth making sure Nalanni would get to live out her destiny. He was actually sent to earth several years before her birth to make sure her destiny would be realized, and for that purpose only. The universe had selected Nalanni before Keith and Nakol new that Nakol was pregnant. At the time of her conception, Nalanni was selected to be the savior of mankind. James Harris was selected to be her guardian at that same moment. Most would call him a guardian angel.

Chapter 19

At the Langdon house all was quiet. Damon was extremely relieved to get to the house without being followed. I had come into the living room to meet him in the front of the house. The girls were in the backyard playing. Kendra sat in the backyard in the shade of the gazebo. I had built it for my mother about five years before she passed.
There is a fish pond with some small Japanese Koi in it. It had a small waterfall that gave my mother many soothing spring and summer day naps as she sat under the gazebo and listened to the running water.
Kendra was feeling its relaxing and therapeutic force as I have caught her dozing off a few times.
The girls played under the orange tree which is always filled with oranges. Paris always

took time to play with Nalanni. They played with Barbie dolls or just read books to each other. Nalanni was an avid reader. Once she learned to read, she wanted to read everything. But for now they just played with the Barbie Dolls. They had the Barbie Hotel and swimming pool out. They played so well together. There was a time when I worried about Paris becoming a teen and not wanting to play with her little sister. Now we have bigger concerns for the both of them. Somehow my baby girl was tied to something big, something very big.

As I met Damon in the living room, I immediately ask him what's going on. He sat down on the couch and began to tell me how he had been follow by someone in a gray late model sedan. He had managed to lose them on 65th street and Normandie Avenue. He went on to explain how he thought someone had been in his house because one of the locks on the backdoor was unlocked. He then told me that he couldn't see inside the car because the windows were tinted too dark. All he was able to see was at least two shadows in the front seats of the car. He had thought his pursuers were police officers, but was not sure because he lost them. He was very hysterical and anxious. I tried to get him to calm down so we could figure out our next move. I asked him if he was sure that he wasn't followed. He said he had sat in the car for a few minutes to see if the car that had been following him or any other car pulled up or came into sight. He saw nothing so he came inside.

Chapter 20

James Harris sat at the chicken restaurant on the corner of 83rd and Western Boulevard waiting to make his connection with our family. He needed us to know the severity of the situation.

Nalanni would recognize him because of her mother's dreams. Her mother often dreamed about the events of her child's future and knew she was important to mankind. She never mentioned anything to me because I would not believe her.

Harris didn't have our house in sight. At the moment he didn't need to. View of the house was not important at this time. Deciding how to approach the house was the growing but delicate situation. The connection had to be made, and now was the time.

He drove out of the north parking lot of the restaurant and made a left onto 83rd street heading west towards the our house. The light was red. He looked at his partner to his right, and his partner looked at him at the same time. His partner Jason Tyler hardly spoke a word. He was not there to talk. His job was to assist James Harris. The light turned green and they proceeded across Western Blvd towards our house. They pulled up to the house. Damon and I never noticed them coming.

Harris and Tyler both got out of the car. Hearing the car doors slam, Damon and I jumped to our feet to look out the window. "Shit, that's the car that was following me!" said Damon.

"Are you sure?"

"Hell yes I'm sure!"

I recognized one of the men. It was the man that had been at every incident. Why was he here, at my home? My first thought was to grab the girls and Kendra and make a break through the backyard and over the brick wall. I needed to talk to this man and now he's here right at my front door. I asked for it and now he's here. I'm not going to let this chance slip away. Damon cautioned me not to open the door. I explained to him that we needed answers, and the answers needed to come from him, James Harris. Damon understood but didn't really agree. He said he would be right behind me, and he was, with his 10mm in his hand and held at his waist. I went to the door and opened it.

There was a bar door which I left closed and locked.

James Harris asked, "May we come in Mr. Langdon?"

"Who are you and what are you doing here?"

"I believe you know who I am already Mr. Langdon. This is not our first meeting. We met on a very important day in your life. A day of happiness and grief. A day that gave the human race hope."

As I listen to him speak the horror of the night Nalanni was born and my wife Nakol died hit me in the heart like a sharp dagger. I felt my knees buckle a little. Damon noticed and quickly grabbed me from behind to keep me from falling. Tears started to well up in my eyes as my mind journeyed back through that night in full detail. I was remembering that night as if it were happening all over again. I was back in the emergency delivery room with Nakol and then back in the waiting room with........ I snapped out of the trans and knew without a doubt who was at my door.

"You're James Harris or Jay for short as you so eloquently put it. I met you the night my wife died and Nalanni was born. You were there at every important event in Nalanni's life."

"Not all, just the public incidents."

"Why the public incidents?"

"May we please come inside to discuss this?

Mr. Langdon we are on your side."

"Ok first tell me who you really are and what roll do you play in all this weird shit that's happening?"

"You must understand Mr. Langdon, that this is not a roll I'm playing. I am carrying out my duty which is my purpose here on earth."

"Your duty? Purpose here on earth? What the hell is all this and what mental joint did you escape from?"

"I'm from another galaxy. My planet no longer exist because of the Ebulliti. They are beings that invade other planets to harvest their natural resources and move on. But in this case the natural resource is your whole planet. But that's not it. What they want here is far more devastating than you could imagine. With the support of your world leaders we have found refuge here on this planet. Your world has kept our existence here a secret for the last eleven years. The Ebulliti didn't know we were here until about two years ago. They sent a probe ship into your atmosphere. Once they were in your atmosphere they were able to detect our being. But for a reason we have just discovered, they were unable to enter your atmosphere. They cannot live very long in your atmosphere without a host. They can only invade children's bodies because their will is not strong enough to fight them off. They target the kids with low self-esteem or kids whose parents used drugs during conception or during pregnancy. Once inside they merge with the host's DNA. All of the host's primary body functions remain intact. They eat, sleep, move around, talk, and communicate with their parents all the same. There are some that fight because they have become aware for some reason. When this happens the invader shows itself to the host in a reflection and the consequences are not good."

"Why, what happens?"

"First the host tries to tell people what's going on with them. People often think they are crazy and submit them to psychological evaluation. Your government has a system that alerts them when a patient exhibits certain characteristics. They watch for certain signs like; saying they're possessed, they see a monster instead of their own reflection when they look into a mirror, or they say things like; a demon made them do it. Those are the basic signs they look for. They then step in and take over from there."

"What do they do with them?"

"They are sent to a special unit inside Juvenile Hall."

"How do you know so much about this?"

"It is our purpose here to track, watch, and terminate if possible all life forms threatening the existence of your daughter, Nalanni."

We have people in place at these facilities to

alert us when an Ebulliti is present or has been present in a host.

"Are there any other consequences we should know about?"

"Yes. The most dangerous. A child that becomes aware that something is inside of him. Instead of being frightened, they embrace the entity inside them and tries to carry out and objective."

"What objective is that?"

"To kill Nalanni if they can or anybody that may help her in the present or future."

"Do you remember the incident at one of your high schools Mr. Langdon?"

"Yes I remember. A kid went in and shot the school up."

"That's what your government want you to think. A child, actually two rejected the Ebulliti after most of the children were Xeroxed at a school assembly in the gymnasium. They knew those children were no longer human but were Ebulliti. They were trying to kill the Ebulliti."

Well, I would like to see them try and kill my baby.

"I'll travel to the end of the galaxy and kill every alien along the way to my keep girls safe and I will risk my life doing it if I have to. They don't know the extent a man will go to, to keep his kids safe. But they are about to find out."

The look on my face must have be that of

disbelief, because Harris told me not to be
shocked because this has been going on for
several years. He went on to explain.

He told me that every time there was a crisis
where kids were killing their parents or
parents killing their children, then
committing suicide were all Ebulliti related.
You here about these kinds of things
happening all the time. You just follow what
the media reports. Your media is controlled
by your government. But you already know
that now, don't you?

"Like I said before, government or not, I
will give my life for those two little girls in
there!

The look on their faces never change as I
explained how far I was willing to go to
keep Nalanni and Paris safe from the
Ebulliti. Harris looked at his partner then
turned back to me and said without any
emotions, "That's what it might take."

I gave him a look as if to say, oh well let's
do it. The truth is I really would travel
anywhere to save her and her sister Paris
safe from these invaders. But somehow, I
think they knew that.

"Mr. Langdon, so far we have contained
almost every event where they have tried
mass possessions. There are some we didn't
get to take care of because the transference
signature was inadequate."

"Transference signature? What do you think
caused that?"

"This usually occurs when a single possession takes place. The host is usually an adult because they are easier to find alone and have more resources. They have minimal restrictions on their availability to travel and move around."

"Are you guys aliens also?"

"Yes we are."

"So that's why you're in the bodies that you're in now. Nobody would question an adult traveling alone or the time in which they chose to travel. No restrictions and not really any questions either."

"That's correct."

"Why are you so interested in saving our planet, you are not even in our galaxy?"

When I asked James Harris that question he went to the trunk of the gray sedan. He pulled out a shiny, metal plate around 12 inches x 12 inches. Harris gestured for me to walk around to the back of the car. He placed the metal plate on top of a glass, three pronged, and trophy looking device. When Harris placed the metal plate on the trophy like object the plate starts to glow. It appeared that we were transported to another world. My house, the gray sedan, the street, and all the houses on the block were gone. We were now floating above another world being obliterated. The devastation was seemingly being done by derelict beings. The damage was being done but it was not clear who or what was causing it. We just watched two minutes of explosions and their homes being destroyed. There was strange plant life and mountains being destroyed. I just watched with amazement.

Although I've seen these things with my own eyes, it still felt like I was in a bad episode of the Twilight Zone. It's still hard to believe that my five year old daughter is, or will be responsible for saving the human race or perhaps the universe. As Jay continued to describe how the Ebulliti were possessing the bodies of children. I wanted to know why the kids with drug habits or self-esteem issues, so I asked.

"Why do they get the kids with drug habits they got from their parent's neglect and self-esteem problems?"

He answered the question before I could get it all out. It was as if he knew what I was going to ask before I asked the question.

Remaining calm as usual he went on to explain. "Like the adults here on earth, the children go through stress periods in their lives. When a human child is stressed out for whatever reason, their brain identifies with the stress and the body produces an enzyme called Cerebrotonin that helps the child deal with this stress level to keep them from shutting down completely. They may behave unruly, some violently, some hyper active, and some just have temper tantrums. These are the ones that produce the enzyme

Cerebrotonin at a higher percentage. The children that do not produce enough of the enzyme shut down. After they shut down, some don't speak, eat, sleep or move around much. The Ebulliti do not want the children that exhibit these behaviors. Have you noticed how calm your daughters are remaining through all that has been happening around them?"

"Yes, they are quite calm, despite what's been going on."

"Your other daughter is calm as well. She acts as if she knows the severity of the situations unfolding around her, and knows she must be or should I say needs to be. Your daughter is either very strong or she must have blended Nalanni's blood with hers at sometime.

My mind quickly went back to the moment when they were playing in the backyard and Nalanni got hurt and Paris cut her own hand and pressed their cuts together. Nalanni then said, "Now I am in you and you are in me. That's when it happened. Nalanni's DNA had merged with Paris'. The effects are showing in Paris' behavior. She's more calm than usual. She don't even argue with her little sister any more, and she's acting as if there is nothing going on. She and Nalanni must communicate quite often. It's like she knows what's going on at the same time Nalanni does. They are becoming closer, as if they realized they are going to have to become as one in order to be a stronger force.

Chapter 21

James Harris quickly changed subjects as if he remembered something of the utmost importance. He went on to say that he was tracking a potential threat that was also tracking Nalanni. The Ebulliti had gotten close at the park but Nalanni was more powerful than they expected. The potential threat was in human form and could be very dangerous. Nalanni would be able to defeat it easily as long as she knows that it's coming in time. This is the only one that James Harris and his comrades did not get to eradicate at the restaurant incident. What made this threat so dangerous is that they didn't know what it looks like, but they did know it was a child.

I asked was the child a boy or girl. Jay responded, "It's a male, human child."

"Do you know about how old he is?"

"He's the age of the girl, Nalanni."

I found it very curious, as to how a small child is getting from place to place. So I asked, "How is a five year old getting around Los Angeles?"

"The Ebulliti are resourceful. They have what we call retainers."

"Retainers? What are they? Are they aliens also?"

"They are indeed all human. But they have made a decision to serve the Ebulliti. The Ebulliti Xerox a copy of their purpose here on earth to the minds of those that are week and can be easily persuaded. Once there intentions are shown to a human, they either accept or reject it. If rejected, they remain alive but they will never have the total functions of their brain. If the Xeroxing process is successful, the Ebulliti's intentions will be imprinted in the minds of the subjects and they will become retainers."

"How are they able to do this?"

"We are not knowledgeable about the full capabilities of their technology. But we do know that, once Xeroxed they will stop at nothing to carry out or help carry out the Ebulliti's objectives to their death."

The horror of the fact that there are forces out to end my daughter's life sent a cold, chilling sense of urgency through mind that resonated in the core of my being. I had gotten over that fact that something strange was happening but now fear and paranoia crept up my spine and over my skin like a light electrical current. My family was in danger, and I knew I would not let anything happen to them as long as I had blood flowing through my veins. The Ebulliti don't know the extent a human father would go to protect his family.

Jay talked about what was coming, but never said once how to stop it once it was here. We need to know how to stop them so we can help Nalanni defeat them. No matter how many special powers she has, she's only a five year old little girl and she is going to need our help.

Chapter 22

Young Kyle Massey had been traveling for days now. His diet was that of any normal five year old. He is tired and needs to somewhere to rest. His protector Mr. Findley has decided to take to a place he feels will be safe for the young child. Mr. Findley knows what needs to be done to achieve the outcome they desire. Young Kyle was chosen for a purpose just as Nalanni. His young body is changing, changing into something he can't control. His raw meat diet is only delaying the inevitable while keeping him strong and alive. Although he lavishes in the devouring the warm red meat, his small body needs something more. Something that will satisfy what lust he's holding back for. So for now his diet must remain as it is. Eat, rest, and wait for now.

The desire for human flesh is becoming to strong for the young Ebulliti. His need for warm flesh is starting to interfere with his ability to hide inside his human vessel. He has been inside the human vessel far too long and needs meat. Human meat. Once human flesh is ingested by him, the metamorphosis will begin within a few hours. He needed to ingest the human flesh but it has to be done at the right time. He needs to be close to his target when the metamorphosis takes place. He needs to be close to "Her." He needs to be able to strike quick, for she will definitely see him coming. He will be stronger than her physically which will work in his favor to defeat and kill the human child.

He's as close as he needs to be to her right now. He's safe with his protectors. The four protectors he has watching over him have proven to be most helpful, especially Mr. Findley the owner of the old 5th Avenue Movie Theater where he now hides and waits. More will join them in the hours to come. When the time comes, his four man army would have grown to at least a couple dozen.

The old abandoned theater is dark, dusty, musty and not a good place for a child to be.

But Kyle Massey is no longer an ordinary child. It's a matter of, if any child still exists in him.

The meat hungry child lies in wait for the chance to feed on human flesh and to end the life of Nalanni. Feeding on the young Nalanni's flesh will be like being rewarded for a job well done. He's been feeding on small animals to hold off the desire of actual human flesh. The retainers have been catching cats and dogs for him to feed on until the time is right, perfectly right. For if Kyle were to feed on human flesh to soon the change would take place too soon and Nalanni would be able to sense him and the element of surprise would be lost and the mission failed. It would be nearly impossible for Kyle to defeat Nalanni. For she would surely kill him.

One of Kyle's retainers enters the once highly operational back office of the old 5th Avenue Theater on Manchester. It is dusty, poorly lit, and cluttered with boxes. Old posters of Rocky, The Karate Kid, and Critters still hang on the brimstone colored walls. A rust, brown, and tan colored, plaid, burlap, couch that had been there for the managers relaxing and philandering was cleared of dust and boxes and was now the resting place of Kyle. Kyle had worked his way to the old theater with the help of his retainers. He posed as the little brother of the teenaged male and female retainers Rob & Kristy. The two posed as Mr. Findley's grandchildren. Their plan worked to get Kyle to the theater. No one bothered to question them. The perfect travel cover: a grandfather and his grandchildren, no one ever suspected them.

Kyle needed to be there in the old theater for a few more days until the right time and opportunity presented itself. Kyle knew he would need more help, so he has summoned more of his retainers so the death of Nalanni would be a success. Over the next thirty six hours, close to two dozen retainers showed up at the theater. All of whom are trying to help Kyle kill Nalanni.

Dozens of retainers now congregate in the 5th Avenue Theater, several of which have just arrived. The theaters was now more crowded and still cluttered from the excess furniture and boxes that were never removed. A female retainer that had been trying to bring a meal to Kyle suddenly tripped over a box. Her head struck the edge of the metal desk that had been left behind by the previous occupants. She then fell and cut her hand on the glass from the old poster frames. Her head was bleeding from the cut she acquired when her head struck the corner of the desk. Kyle was no more than ten feet from teenaged girl. He saw the cut on her arm and the blood on her head. The blood from the cut was dripping profusely.

The commotion from the fall had caused Kyle to rise up from his rest. The blood from the teen's injuries caught his sight and held it. He was captivated by the sight and smell of the blood. The metallic smell of blood along with the cherry red color of the blood was sending Kyle into an uncontrollable rage. His eyes were starting to turn a bright orange. His pupils had dilated down to the size of the tip of a ball point pen. His teeth changed shape. His once so called baby teeth had turned into that of a large piranha. Blue veins ran through his face like a map and his breathing had become hard and rugged like that of a wild animal. His focus was solely on the blood that dripped from the retainer's hand. The hunger for human flesh was now in control. Little Kyle Massey was no longer present. The time was not right. Feeding on human flesh right now would cause the metamorphosis to take place soon after, and the plan to kill the one person that could actually stop them would be jeopardized. The hunger was too strong. He needed to feed and he needed to feed now!

Chapter 23

My mind went back to the thought of all the killings that have taken place over the years. All the child on child deaths, the parents that kill their children, and the children that had kill their parents, were all suspect of being Ebulliti involved.

The question still remains, how do we stop them? Can they be shot and killed, or do we have to perform some sort of ritual I thought as Harris and his partner left the house. I needed to know so I ran out the door and to his car. I managed to stop them before they drove off. I hit him with the question, "How do I kill them?"

James Harris rolled down the window and said, "Shoot them in the heart or sever the head."

"But they are just kids!" I said.

"They are not kids. They aren't even human any longer. Once the Ebulliti have been in their bodies for more than an hour they are dead and cannot be saved. So for the sake of Nalanni don't view them as being human, because the moment you do, you, Paris, Nalanni and the rest of the world is dead. We cannot let that happen!" *(His voice was strong and firm)*

After he spoke those words calmly and then he drove away.

The gray sedan disappeared up 83rd street going west towards Inglewood.
The sun still hang high in the western sky and would soon descend and disappear over the horizon of roof tops.

I knew in my heart that the words he spoke were the honest truth. There was no time and room for underestimating the Ebulliti. They were here for a purpose, and that purpose happens to be the demise of my five year old daughter Nalanni. She needs me, and the rest of us for that matter. I am not going to let her down! I just can't and I won't!

I heard the bar door close on the porch behind me. Paris had been standing there during my conversation with Jay. I'm not sure if she heard the conversation, or what she saw when we seemed to be transported to another world, but I know she heard the part about not taking the Ebulliti too lightly for it would mean the death of her sister, whom she loves dearly.
I stood curbside for about fifteen seconds after I heard the bar door close. I still hadn't come to grip with the idea that my five year old daughter was going to be responsible for saving the world and maybe the universe.
A small worried voice came from behind me saying, "So daddy, what are we going to do to save my sister and the world?" Paris had

crept up behind me. Her words came out to me as if she was really expecting an answer. I did hear the bar door close but I didn't hear any footsteps. She was just all of a sudden standing behind me. I knew for sure now that she heard some of my conversation with Jay. Paris was never the aggressive type but always loyal and trustworthy for a young girl. She loves her sister and appeared to be ready to fight for her is she has to. I turned to her and said, "I'm not sure. But I know I have to figure something out."

As I was saying those words I turned and gave my oldest daughter a loving hug that was meant to say, I got you. I got the both of you and that everything will be alright. Paris hugged me around my waste and looked up at me with those pretty green eyes and said, "That's what Nalanni keeps saying to me."

I said, "What? That we have to figure something out?"

She said, "No. That you got us, and everything will be alright."

"But I never said that. I just thought it."

"Yes you did dad. I heard you loud and clear."

"No I...."

I stopped in the middle of my sentence. I thought about Paris and Nalanni's ability to communicate with each other telepathically. Maybe they can read my thoughts as well. I thought about, how many of my thoughts could they actually hear. I quickly checked myself for over analyzing my every thought. We started walking side by side towards the porch. My right arm hugged her around her neck and my hand rested on her shoulder. She was holding me around my waste with her hands interlocked. As we reach the edge of the porch, Nalanni was standing their waiting for us. As I reached the top of the porch, Nalanni said calmly, "Daddy, I can hear everything and Paris only hears what she needs to hear."

Feeling kind of shocked by what Nalanni just said, I raised my left eye brown and gave a look as to say, oh is that right. We went inside the house. Kendra was preparing dinner for us.

It's amazing how everybody is holding up and going their days as if somewhat normal. I guess trying to remain normal through all of this Sci-Fi chaos is what we need to keep from losing it.

Chapter 24

In Inglewood the situation was getting out of order. Kyle was losing control, and fast. His hunger for human flesh was becoming dominant over the need to repress his hunger so the end game of killing Nalanni could be achieved. A retainer, probably the most trusted servant of his tried to calm him down. He immediately had the girl removed from the room where Kyle was. Having the girl removed from the room proved to be what was needed to curve Kyle's lust to taste human flesh.

He immediately turned and grabbed the remainder of a cat that had been brought to him earlier to feed on. Although he fed on it like a wild animal, his breathing calmed as he fed on the fairly fresh cat carcass. His teeth and eyes returned almost too normal. He seemed to be back in control of himself, at least for now. Mr. Findley realized that Kyle was losing control. He knows Kyle won't be able to hold off the hunger for too much longer. The time to take action was growing all so near. Mr. Findley also knew that if Kyle failed there would be others to take his place for Kyle would no longer be alive to try again. Kyle laid back down on the couch in the abandoned theater. Kyle Massey was now in control again and the Ebulliti still had a chance.

Chapter 25

Kendra prepared a fine dinner for us and insisted that we sit down and have dinner together. I don't remember her being a great cook. She had cooked meals for me while we were dating but not to this extent. She prepared baked chicken that was juicy and seasoned to perfection. Steamed broccoli soaked in butter, baked potatoes, macaroni &cheese, and dinner rolls topped off the menu for the evening. Everything looked, smelled, and tasted great.

Damon started a conversation at the table about James Harris. He asked what Harris had to say about everything. I tried to gesture to him to not bring it up in the presence of the girls. Nalanni not once looking up from her plate said, "It's ok dad we don't mind."

Damon said, "How does she do that? She never looked up at you."
Kendra quickly replied, "Women's intuition."
Nalanni and Paris both with food in their mouths turned to each other and smiled. Kendra looked at me, shrugged her shoulders and joined the girls in their smile. I was waiting for a sarcastic remark from Paris that never came. She continued to eat her dinner. Paris never passed up a chance to emit sarcasm from her mouth at the expense of her sister. I just stared at her with a smirk on my face and my eyebrows raised. "Wow," I thought. She really has changed.
Damon looked at me and said, "Anyway bro. How do we kill them?"
Nalanni answered for me, "That's easy. Remove the head and the body will fall. Oh, and you can use fire."
"Fire?" said Damon.
"Yeah, you know like, burn them." both the girls replied with sarcasm.
Everybody turned and looked at the girls with concern as to how they knew about killing the Ebulliti. In any normal situation, this information would be disturbing coming from a young child. But these are not normal times. Far from normal!
My mind grasped the concept and stored the information for future reference. Cut off the head or burned them was filed. The fact that this information came from my five year old

daughter still disturbed me, regardless of the times. We now have a way to fight them once we encounter them. This new knowledge of ways to kill the Ebulliti gave me a sigh of relief even if for just a brief moment.

I continued to eat my delicious dinner that Kendra cooked for us. The conversation about how to kill the Ebulliti ended just as quickly as it started. Everybody just dug their faces down into their plates so they finish their dinner. Paris finished eating her dinner and asked for some desert. Nalanni quickly said she was finished even though she wasn't so she could get some pie. Damon and I decided to skip desert so we could go out in the yard to talk strategies to prevent or counteract any attacks on Nalanni and ourselves.

The night was slightly warm, about 78 degrees. We pulled up a couple of lawn chairs that had been given to me by a fellow roller pigeon fancier. the green and white striped pillows on the actual metal frame comfortable. Before all of this alien and my daughter saving the world crap I had been an avid roller pigeon flyer and breeder. I would spend hours in my pigeon loft watching my rollers in my loft during the night and flying them during the daylight hours. They served as a sort of therapy to the hustle and bustle of being a single parent in today's society. I would go out to the loft, and for those brief minutes that I was in there, my worries would disappear or I would think of ways to settle problems. My late wife Nakol often complained about me spending so much time with the birds but then she would say, well at least I was at home and not at a bar or strip club. I loved her for that. I had put her through so much during our marriage. It was to my surprise that she stayed with me for so long. I hate the fact that I spent so much time on meaningless people and things. All that time I wasted could have been spent with the woman I really loved and not frolicking around LA in the company of other women. What a waste. When I got my act together we had a few happy years and then she was gone. I wouldn't trade those last years anything.

Damon asked me how would we burn them if we came across one of the Ebulliti, or several at a time. What would people think if we went around town torching young kids and teenagers? We would probably be marked as murderers and hunted down by every law enforcement agency. Most people are unaware that the Ebulliti even exist. We can't go around screaming, "Deadly Aliens are taking over kids bodies." For we would surely be in the Augusta Hawkins Mental Hospital. So I thought we needed to find a way to expose them and keep my girls safe at the same time. The fact that the government already knows they are here makes our task harder. Any attempts by us to make the Ebulliti's existence here on earth public, could and most likely would be covered up by the US Government and us in danger. We are on our own in this and we have to be ready to make a stand if necessary and to do that we needed weapons. Serious weapons!

Chapter 26

Kyle was calm now but the other Ebulliti
were getting stronger in numbers all over
Los Angeles and neighboring cities. There
were takeovers in Compton, Gardena,
downtown Los Angeles, and other cities
where there are poverty stricken children.
The guardians were not able to ward off or
rectify all of the takeovers due to their
shortness in numbers. I never knew how
many suffering youth we have here in Los
Angeles, neighboring cities, and counties.

The numbers are staggering. The growing numbers in Ebulliti could get to overwhelming numbers. My attempt to protect my daughter is growing more and more unlikely. The feeling of failing was haunting my brain. I couldn't shake it. It's was growing stronger and stronger and I didn't know what to do. I grabbed my head from the sides and everything started spinning. I was sweating profusely and my head was now pounding. It felt like I was losing my mind. Then it got dark.

All of a sudden I was I was in a large room. The room was well lit. There were fluorescent lights across the top of all four walls right at the ceiling. There was no door, no windows, no nothing, just me, the dull gray walls, cold cement floor, and the lights. I ran around the room franticly searching for an exit or something. I started spinning in circles clockwise looking at the ceiling, at least it felt like I was spinning. When I settle down I knew that I wasn't spinning. It was the room. When the room stopped spinning I was on my back. I sat up on the floor with my legs straight out in front of me. There was someone standing directly in front of me against the dull gray wall. The image was blurry at first. When it became clear I recognized the person standing there. The person stood there saying nothing at first. My first thought was, what the hell is he doing here?! Then I thought, how did he get in here? Harris just stood there with this grin on his face, which seemed kind of odd because he shows no emotions on his face at all. I sat there on the floor confused. "What's going on here?" I said.

Still nothing from Harris. I slowly got up off the floor but did not approach or attempt to approach Harris. As a matter of fact, I took a few steps back. Harris' face changed. The grin on his face turned an outright smile. He stopped smiling, looked my right in my face and said, "Things are not always as they seem."

And just like that he was gone. I looked around at all four walls. Harris was gone. Oh shit! The room started shaking, the humming started, the temperature dropped, and the ceiling opened up. The eyes came straight at me like a flash.

"Keith! Keith! Wake up!" I heard a voice yelling out at me. All of a sudden the room was no longer spinning, my headache was gone, and all of the feelings of despair were no longer in my brain. I opened my eyes to see the ceiling and Kendra staring down at me with her hands on my shoulders shaking me.

In a confused state I asked, "What happened? What's going on?"

"You were dreaming." said Kendra.

"Dreaming? When did I go to sleep?"

"But it seemed so real. I don't even

remember going to bed. How long was asleep?"

"You were sleep for a whole day."

"What happened to me; was I drunk or something?"

"You and Damon were outside in the backyard talking, and when you came in you said you were tired and went straight to bed."

"I don't remember ever going to bed. All I remember is eating dinner and talking to Damon about getting weapons to fight the Ebulliti."

"You were having a conversation with someone. Mostly mumbling though. Who were you talking to?"

With a look of confusion I said, "I don't know."

The truth of the matter is, I didn't know what had transpired over the last twenty four hours. All I knew was we needed weapons, and some serious ones at that. I have no idea where to get weapons such as the ones we need to kill the Ebulliti. No idea.

I remembered having a conversation with Harris but I don't know when or where this conversation took place. Just shrugged my shoulders and dismissed the thought.

Chapter 27

As we sit here stuck trying to figure out where to get the weapons to fight the Ebulliti, they are getting stronger in numbers. Damon was sitting at the kitchen table when I walked into the kitchen. He looked up at me as I walked in as if to say, about time you snapped out of it. I had been sleep for a full twenty four hours and had no recollection of the whole night or just before I actually fell asleep. Damon asked me a question that didn't sit well with me. He asked if I found the answer to our problems in my dreams. He was being his usual sarcastic self. Just as I was about to answer him, Nalanni said from behind me, "He already knows where to get the weapons you need Uncle Damon, and so do you."

"Oh yeah? And where might that be?" I said to her as I turned around to see my baby girl giving me more advice.

"Check your friends, one in particular. You'll find him most helpful." then she politely turns and walks away. Her tone was abnormal, as if someone else was inside her body.

"Bro, man, I know she's my niece, but she's freaking me the fuck out. What's up with her?"

"Chill out Damon, she's alright."

After she made her statement, Nalanni turned and walked back into the living room with Paris to watch TV.

I went outside to my pigeon loft. I needed to think, and there is no other place I do that better than my pigeon loft. Nalanni said, *"Check your friends, one in particular."*

My mind kept going over that statement. Over and over it ran through my mind as I watched my birds go about their mating and breeding rituals. It's the middle of summer and they are at the height of their breeding. The cock birds are driving the hens to nest. Others are feeding their squabs.

Then it hit me. The person, "Sidewinder" just popped into my head. I hadn't talked to Sidewinder since my hustling days over fifteen years ago. I may not have talked to him but I'm sure Damon has.

I ran out of the loft and into the house. I started calling Damon's name before I got to the back door. I snatched open the back door and yelled his name again, "Damon!"

"What?" he answered.

"I know what to do. I mean I know who can help us!" I said with much excitement and enthusiasm.

"Who?" said Damon.

"Sidewinder."

Although I hadn't talked to him in years, I knew he was our only hope. Damon kept in contact with him due to his dealings in the street.

Sidewinder was once a close friend of mine when I sold drugs in the streets. He has many connections that can help us in our fight with the Ebulliti. He has a warehouse in the hood that has everything from assault rifles to zip guns. Well, it's not an actual warehouse. It's more like a basement, a large basement that had been reinforced to keep out thieves and the police. It has three inch steel walls and ceiling, 4 inch steel doors that are reinforced to withstand any kind of gun fire or grenade attack. It has an emergency escape route. A tunnel that travels under the street for three blocks and comes up in a home that is owned by Sidewinder but occupied by some of his workers.

Sidewinder may be our only hope of getting the weapons we need. Getting the weapons may not be the problem. It's the cost that I'm worried about. I decided that we had to meet with Sidewinder, and soon.

Damon called Sidewinder from his cell phone to set up the meeting. He walked away from me to keep me from hearing the conversation.

While Damon was in the living room talking on the phone I stayed in the kitchen leaning on the counter. Kendra and the girls quietly watched TV in the back bedroom. She was good to the girls and they liked her very much. Her relationship with them was natural. It's what they needed in their lives at this time. I also needed her as much as the girls did and maybe more. She's good, good for all of us.

Damon returned to the kitchen. He had been on the phone for all of about two minutes. Damon said Sidewinder wanted to meet with us now at the warehouse. I'm sure he didn't use the word warehouse. He most likely said, "The Spot." He always speaks in codes when on the phone in fear that the police or FEDS were listening.

We pulled up to The Spot. The Spot is in the basement of and old but large redecorated house on 71st street in Los Angeles. That house had been recently stucco and texture coated. It was painted a tan like color with a coco brown trimming. The original windows had been replaced with new double pane glass windows. The yard was well groomed and no one seemed to be there. I knew that wasn't the case at all.

I asked Damon where everybody was. He said, "Believe me; they've been watching us as soon as we turned on the block."

Which was true. He has lookouts sitting in cars parked in driveways at both ends of the blocks. The corner houses on Normandie Avenue and both the corner houses on Haldale. He also has a few soldiers that walk the block heavily armed. The guys that were at both ends of the block were heavily armed with AK47 assault rifles along with handguns. Because it was dark we never noticed them. Damon already knew they were there. A tall black man came out of the house and said, "Come on. Side is waiting for yal."

We looked at each other and proceeded to follow the gentleman. He turned and looked at Damon and said, "What up dog? Where you been?"

"Cuz, I been dealing with some wicked shit out here."

"You shudda hit us up cuz, we got yo back."

"Fo sho my nig."

Damon and the guy stopped and gave each other some homie love in the form of a one armed hug with a fist tap to the back and a hand shake at the same time. He led us to a closet door. The closet was large but had a false wall in the back behind some hanging clothes that opened up to reveal a large steel door. There were cameras pointing at the door, and outside the closet door. There are probably cameras all through the house. We then stepped down 13 steps to a section where there were surveillance monitors to the left in a 10ftx10ft room the showed 12 different locations throughout the house and yard. We stepped down 10 more steps and into what appeared to be a warehouse for real. This couldn't be the size of just this single house. It looked like it extended well into the backyard and maybe the house behind, and it actually did. For the end of the warehouse was under the house on the next block. We walked through many boxes that were stacked up to the top which was about 8 feet high. There were flat screen TV'S, CD players, blue ray players, computers, desk and laptops, and much more. It was like a small Costco. We didn't go all the way to the back but veered to the right through a tight space of boxes where we came to an opening. The opening was about 6" x 10" with its own lighting system. He turns on the lights with a flip of a switch that was on the wall to his right. There was a regular looking flat wall in front of us. He walked up to the wall and said, "Open says me." which I thought was rather cliché.

The doors split down the middle revealing a room with nothing but weapons and ammunition. My eyes quickly scanned the room for the type of weapons we can use for our fight. I looked to the left, then to the right, on the top shelf, bottom shelves, and then I saw a crate that was covered.

I asked, "What's under there?"

Side said, "Oh those are my babies."

When I asked what they are, he pulled back the canvas and opened the crate. When he

pulled one out, I said, Hell yes, that's what
I'm talking about!"
In the crate were flame thrower guns. We
took two of them and couple of machetes.
I know now that we have a chance to help
Nalanni fight the Ebulliti.

Chapter 28

With a new found sense of security Damon
and I headed back to the house with the
flame guns in the trunk and ready to rock
and roll with the Ebulliti. I was surprised at
the fact that Side let me take them without
actually working out a price first. He always
sets a price. He said he was letting me take
the weapons because I asked. The fact that I
had came to him signaled to him that I really
needed them for a serious purpose. He knew
that I would not go to him unless it was for
something serious. We were once business
partners. When I chose the family life and
left the street game, he felt I had turned my
back on him. I turned my back on that life
and chose life with my wife and kids. He
couldn't understand my decision, or he
didn't want to understand it. There comes a
time in a man's life when he must choose a
road to follow, and that was the time in my
life and the choice I made was the best for
my family and I.
My brother Damon didn't understand my
decision either. He felt like I was
abandoning him and leaving him all alone in

the streets of LA. I had asked him to come along with me. We both had enough money to leave the game for good. Damon was hooked on the life and was not interested in leaving the game. I had just married the woman of my dreams and was planning on starting a family with her. My priorities had to change and right at that moment. I knew in my heart and soul that, if I didn't get out when I did, I would have been forever stuck in the game, in jail, or dead. I always paid attention to that little voice inside me, because every time I didn't, something bad happened to me. My gut told me to get out of the game and marry Nakol, and I did.

Chapter 29

The 55th Street Boys and Girls club had been a refuge for children for over fifty years. Children not only went there for sports, but for several other programs that the club offered. Today there are over one hundred children on site. The summer program is in full swing and full of kids. Most of the children are in the gymnasium attending a summer league basketball game. There are children, coaches, parents, and club staff inside the gym. Since the gym had been reconstructed a state of the art air conditioning system, the doors were closed to the outside air. The 88degree heat was outside and the gym remained cool. The teams that were playing appeared to be in the age range of 9 - 10 years old. A few parents started complaining about the temperature of the gym. They were saying it was getting too cold in the gym. All over the crowd you could hear people commenting on the temperature in the gym. People were starting to head towards the doors hoping to get outside to the warmth of the summer heat or let some of the heat in the gym. A woman in her late twenties or early thirties tried the west door and it was locked. Another parent walked up and asked, "Why is this door locked?" Deep concern was in her voice. A man tried the north exit and it was locked as well. In less than a minute there were parents at all exits trying to get out of the gym. Staff members rushed to the doors to see why and how they were locked. The doors had no other visible restraints other than those which are built into the doors. A simple push should have released the locking mechanisms on the doors. Parents and staff alike pushed and pushed but the doors remained locked. The exit through the main lobby was also locked. People on the outside of this entrance were trying to get in the gym while the people on the inside were trying to get out. Within a few minutes the game had stopped and there was panic all over the gym. The kids were frightened and some were crying.

The humming started and everybody seemed to stop and look around. When the lights began to flicker everybody looked up towards the ceiling. The humming got even louder, louder than all the other times before. The building shook and it shook with

more intensity also. Screams came from all over the gym, "Earth quake! Earth quake!"
Kids disappeared and reappeared all over the gym. Parents fainted. Everybody in the gym was now on the floor and moving slowly as if coming to after being knocked out. The humming had stopped, the temperature returned to normal, and the doors were unlocked.
The walls and all the solid surfaces were sweating due to the concentration of the cold air meeting the warm air.
People rushed into the gym from the main lobby entrance. They attended to those that were still slowly getting up. They were asking questions about what had just happened. The people all gave the same answer. They all said it got cold, the doors were locked, and there was an earthquake. The people that were helping looked at each other and asked, "What earthquake?"
They had no idea what had happened inside the gym. Everything outside the gym was normal. They just knew the gym doors were locked. They didn't experience the drop in temperature or the earthquake. People were exiting from all exits. Some were shook up and some had recovered.
The Ebulliti had struck again, and everybody was oblivious to what had just happened.

Chapter 30

James Harris pulled up to the Boys and Girls Club to see people leaving form all exits. The chance to control the site had dissipated and there was no chance of tracking down every one that was inside the gym. This was bad! Very bad! Hundreds of new potential threats were now loose in LA. Things were already bad, but now they are worse. Our job to help Nalanni keep the world safe had just gotten harder. No matter how hard the task at hand had gotten, The Guardians were not going to let the Ebulliti take over and destroy the human race. James Harris vowed to protect Nalanni at any cost, even sacrificing his own life to save hers. There were several potential Ebulliti loose in LA, and he is going to track down and kill as many as he could. He knows he can't track them down until they start to change or have changed. He also knows that he won't be able to get them all. But before the hunt began, he had to first contact me and warn me of the events that have just taken place.

My phone rang at about 4:00pm. It was James Harris. He informed of the event that took place at the 55th street Boys and Girls club. He explained to me that there was a massive possession and transference. This latest incident took place at the B&G Club on 55thst.

I thought to myself, shit that place is always loaded with kids. I immediately asked him was he able to solve the problem. My heart was pounding after I asked the question.

And the answer made it pound harder and made my stomach drop. I knew this meant my baby was in more danger now. Fear for my child's life is starting to creep down my spine. Only God knows how many children were there at that crucial time.

All I could say was, "FUCK!"

My yelling must have been heard inside the house because Kendra came out back to see what happened.

She came a few steps outside the door and stopped about a foot in front of the small pond where the little water fall was. I was out back standing near the kit boxes. I was flying a kit of rollers for my enjoyment.

She asked me, "Are you ok?"

I quickly answered, "I'm good. A damn falcon just got one of my birds."

I was actually responding to the information James Harris had just relayed to me.

Kendra said ok and went back inside with the girls. I asked Harris what was his plan to eradicate the incident. He told me he would track down as many as he could and kill them. I asked him how many does he think there are. He said close to a hundred. I just shook my head and thought, "God help us!"

Chapter 31

While Kendra was in the backyard Nalanni
was going through something inside the
house. Within the two to three minutes
Kendra was in the backyard Nalanni had
started sweating. She was in a deep stare and
her skin was on fire. Paris called her name
several times.
Nalanni! Nalanni! Nalanni!
But she did not answer her. They had been
playing the card game Uno. Kendra had
been playing Uno with the girls. She made
her last move before she heard me yell. She
got up quickly and instructed the girls to
continue to play. Paris made her move.
When it was Nalanni's turn to play she just
stared as if she were in a trans like state.
When Nalanni didn't respond to Paris'
attempts to get her attention so she could
take her turn, she got worried. She was
headed towards the backyard when she met
Kendra in the kitchen. Paris was in a hurry.
Kendra sensed that something was wrong
with Paris because she was moving so fast
and the look on face was that of fear or
serious worry. The fact that she was moving
fast and looking for her sent an alarm to her
that something was wrong with Nalanni.

Kendra rushed through the kitchen and down the hall to the room where Nalanni was. Paris continued to the backyard to get me. She burst through the back door screaming daddy, daddy! There is something wrong with Nalanni! I had an old soup can full of pigeon feed in my hand. I dropped it and all the feed in the can fell all over the ground. I use a small soup can to feed my birds when they are finish flying.

I ran in the house asking Paris what's wrong with Nalanni as we ran through the kitchen and down the hall. I got to the room to find Nalanni sitting up on the floor. She was in a sort of trans. Paris' face showed fear for the first time since the restaurant incident. All of a sudden she spoke. While in the trans like state she said, "He'll be coming soon," and passed out. She was out for only a few seconds. When she came too, it was like nothing ever happened. The first thing she said was, "It's my turn." then she said, "Why is everybody staring at me?" we all looked at each other and then quickly back at her. Kendra asked her how she was doing. She said she was fine. Then I asked her did she remember anything. She said, "Like what?"

She didn't remember a thing other than what happened before her trans.

What had caused this episode? And who was, He?

Chapter 32

The atmosphere around the old theater was quiet and somber. None of the retainers were in sight. From across Manchester Boulevard the theater looked to be empty and abandoned, which is exactly as it should look on the outside. On the inside things were not as calm. Kyle had been sleeping until it was time to awaken to carry out his assignment. Kyle's ability to control his hunger for human flesh was proving to be too strong for him to handle. The female that cut herself earlier had been staying away from him until it was time for the big event. Jason Tyler was parked across Manchester Blvd. staking out the old theater. The transference signature was strong. He was able to track the Ebulleti and the retainers to this location. Jason Tyler's observation of the old theater proved to be half right. Most of the retainers were out getting food for Kyle. Only two of them were left to care for Kyle, a young man of about 22 years old and the girl that cut her arm.

Tyler had got a call that several teen aged

kids were going in and out of the old theater. That was all the confirmation he needed to stake out the old theater. Although the owner was seen on site talking to them, a neighbor called in to complain about the young adults hanging around the neighborhood. Several small animals had been reported missing in the neighborhood, so Tyler decided to go check it out while his partner was still checking on leads to find the victims of the B&G Club.

Harris and Tyler used police scanners and radios to monitor police activity. Tyler's vessel was an actual police officer. But he wanted to keep his investigation off the record to avoid detection by government authorities. He was trained in surveillance. Even trained professionals make mistakes. He was walking around the back of the theater through the alley. There was a window a few feet in from the street. There was a pile of wood that seemed to be sturdy enough to stand on. Tyler tried to stand on the pile and slipped. The slip made a small crashing sound, just enough to be heard inside of the theater. The young man inside heard the crash and went to check it out. While he was checking on the crash outside Kyle had awaken and wanted food. The girl was the only one there to take care of his needs at this time. Kyle called to be served. No other person was there to hear him. The girl heard him but tried to act as if she didn't. Kyle was starting to get angry, and as he did he was starting to change. His voice became deep, low and rough. Veins were popping out of his forehead and neck. His skin paled and eyes turned red. He got up to find out why he wasn't being served. He called out once more but no one answered. He lifted his head and nose as if to smell something in the air. He got excited and his heart started beating fast and hard. He smelt something in the air inside the old theater besides the normal stench of mildew and dust, and that something was human blood. He started getting more and more out of control. His hunger was guiding him through the theater with a purpose, and that purpose was to feed. Feed on human flesh!

Outside the theater Tyler had managed to keep out of the site of the young male retainer. He scaled a six foot fence and hid in a yard.

Kyle's hunger was now to strong and he was closing in on his meal. It was still too early for him to feed on the flesh of a human, but he could no longer fight it. His time to feed was now. The girl attempted to hide in an empty office. While going through the door she bumped her hand and started to bleed. The fresh blood threw Kyle into a rage. He closed in on the girl, his breathing strong and rugged, his eyes were blood shot red.

There was nothing to stop him now. He approached the office door. The girl had locked the door from the inside. The door was an old wooden door that was not made to keep people out but to provide privacy only. The door was no match for Kyle's hunger.

CRASH! Kyle was inside the room with the girl. The once three and a half foot boy had mutated to a five foot monster and now has the strength of ten men. The hunger for human flesh had grown so strong in him that he was no longer Kyle. Once inside the room his focus went straight to the blood that was dripping profusely from the bandaged wound. His stare was so intense as he approached her. Sobbing, the girl knew she had nowhere to go and surrendered herself to him.

Chapter 33

The young male retainer looked out the back door to try and see what had caused the noise. He took a couple of steps out the door and look to his left and right down the alley. Other than the pile of wood that was under the window, there was nowhere for anybody to hide. There was a brick wall across the alley that was about six feet high. It's the only place someone could hide if they had too. The retainer walked over to the wall looked over and no one was there. He turned, looked both ways and went back inside the theater. As he locked the door he heard a short scream. It sounded as if it was cut off before the full scream could get out. The retainer went to where the scream had come from only to find his master Kyle devouring the girl like a starved beast.

Kyle at first only licked the blood that was coming from the girl's bandage. The taste of the warm blood had made him so crazy with hunger that the first bite went through her flesh and to the bone like a shark bite. Kyle's mouth was not as big as a shark's but his teeth were as sharp. The next bite severed the arm completely. There were no screams coming from the girls limp, blood soaked body. Kyle had broken her neck when he grabbed her by the neck and arm. She had only gotten out a partial scream then snap went her neck. Kyle was so strong and hunger driven that he snapped her neck and arm on the initial grab. Blood was everywhere in the little office. The walls, floor, and the old desk were cover with warm fresh blood. Kyle had devoured arms, half her torso, and her left thigh before he slowed down. The young male had stepped outside the door but stayed near. There was no need for him to fear Kyle for he had already fed.

There was some commotion coming from the back of the theater. This time it was the others coming back from hunting for Kyle's meal. Too late! As the retainer in charge walked in, he saw the young male standing in the hall outside of the office and knew something had happened. When he looked inside the office to see Kyle sitting in the corner next to the desk and the girls half eaten body on the floor in front of him and the blood everywhere, he knew Kyle would be changing soon. Kyle just sat up in the corner breathing deep, slow in and out breaths. Blood was all over his face, chest, and hands. His eyes had changed from red to a deep glowing orange. He even had a chunk of the girls flesh hanging from his mouth. All he did now was sit there and breathe.

Chapter 34

It has been nearly five hours since the take over at the B&G Club. James Harris had already tracked down and eradicated fourteen Ebulliti. His job was far from over. He just needed to get as many of them as possible. The more he took down means less to worry about later. All of the Ebulliti that he has taken down so far were the players of the teams that were competing earlier that day. He decided to go after them first because they were the easiest to track. He had gotten the names from the scorebook that was left on the scorer's table. Since there was so much commotion he had time to access the team's files in the office also. There he found names and addresses to the players.

Eighteen down and only two more players left. One of these would prove to be a problem.

Khalid Morris, the center for one of the teams was the closest on the list. Khalid was a slender kid about six feet tall. He was taller than the average 12 year old. Khalid was a quiet kid and a hell of an athlete.

Harris drove by the house slowly to make sure there was no one hanging out at the house or outside on the block for that matter. All seemed to be clear, this was his chance. He parked half way down the street under a large hanging willow tree. He sat there for a few moments to observe the house for movement. There was no visible movement from where he sat. He needed a better view of the house. He got out the car and walked pass the Morris home. The records in the file say he has a younger brother. His mother was a single parent, as were most of the kids on the teams. That explained why the B&G Club was targeted. The house across the street appeared to be vacant. It would provide adequate cover for observation. The hedges around the house were thick and had not been groomed in at least four or five months. It appeared that someone attempted to trim the front hedges but did a poor job. Maybe an attempt to please the block club or something. They still were good enough to hide behind and peek through to see the brown house with dark brow trimming. Harris needed to find a way to get a peek into the house. The front of the Morris house was quiet and dark. The whole block was quiet. Harris needed to get around the house to get a better look. The front of the house was clear for the most part, with the exception of a few rose bushes that grew under the picture window. Both sides of the house had an open space. On the right side of the house was the driveway. The left side was only about four feet wide, and was probably used as an alternate entrance to the backyard. Both sides were lined with bushes that lined the fences. The bush was taller on the driveway side and were about seven feet tall. Harris walked half way down the driveway to see if there was anybody up or moving around inside. There were no lights on inside the house on the driveway side. The moon provided adequate light for Harris to maneuver down the side of the house and remain concealed from the neighbors that may be taking a last peek outside before calling it a night. The driveway was fairly clean, which made it easy to maneuver without making any noise. He crept around to the front of the house to the left side. Besides the living room there were two other rooms on this side of the house. The hedges on this side of the house blocked most of the moon light. There was enough space to move with ease down the side of the house without brushing against the bushes. A thin strip of cement went down this side of the house to a locked gate which was an entrance to the backyard. There was a thick layer of shrubbery that flanked the cement walkway to the side opposite the house. Harris made sure he was careful not to get his feet caught and trip on the shrubbery. The element of surprise was on his side and he could not lose this edge. He walked all the way to the back and looked over the gate to get a full view of the backyard. The backyard was neat and roomy. The garage was all the way to the right of the yard. The walkway to the backyard kept on beyond the gate and led into a small orchard of some kind. Someone spends a lot of time back there keeping this groomed very well. A light breeze swept through the orchard. A sweet scent of ripe peaches flirted with Harris' nose and gave hint to the fact that the orchard was full of peach trees. Without that breeze that detail would have not been made clear to him on the account that it was so dark. All in all, the backyard was clear. After he made sure the backyard was clear he started toward the house. No light showed through from the inside of the house to the backyard.

The first room was dark and quiet. There was no apparent threat inside as far as Harris knew. There was no light in this room at all, not even enough to cast a moderate shadow. Harris dismissed this room as being empty. The second room appeared to be glowing. At first glance it appeared to be the light from a television set that was left on. A closer look made it apparent that this was no television light. The light seemed to get brighter as Harris got closer with each step. Carefully making his way through the shrubbery he approached the next window. The light stopped flashing and remains steady. Harris got to the window, looked in and saw someone lying in the bed that was closes to the window on their back. He got closer to the window and seen that it was a small adult or a large kid. Closer observation confirmed that the figure was in fact that of a young male. It was Khalid Morris the oldest of the two boys. His bed was glowing as if the mattress was made out of light. On the bed next to his but against the wall was a child. The child was about the age of 7 or 8. The child had backed up into the corner on his bed hiding his face and crying. He was scared to death. Why was this kid glowing? The Ebulliti don't usually glow during or after transformation. Harris' face was more serious that of which it usually shows. Harris needed to get into the house. He ran to the front of the house. He banged on the front door but there was no answer. He banged even harder but still no answer. He thought the mother would hear and open the door but she never came to the door. Where was the mother? She was not at work he thought because her car was still parked in the drive way. He needed to get in the house and fast. He backed up and kicked the door open. The door busted open with a single kick. He ran through the house to the glowing room. Once inside the room he called out to the smaller child trying to get him to come to him. The bed stopped glowing and now only Khalid was glowing. He started to look like he was changing or transforming into something else. The image looked like an Ebulliti coming out of Khalid's body. Harris knew exactly what was happening now. Khalid's body was rejecting the Ebulliti. His body was driving it out. And with nowhere else to go it would go right after the young boy on the bed. Harris knew what needed to be done but the timing would have to be perfect. He pulled a device that looked like a flash light from his belt. He will only get one chance at this. He had to wait until the Ebulliti was out of Khalid, grab the young boy and fire the light beam at the Ebulliti.

The Ebulliti is half way out of Khalid. Harris has the flashlight like device in his hand.

It's out! Harris grabs the boy, the Ebulliti gets confused and has nowhere to go. The ghostly creature rises to the ceiling, looks at Harris and screams a loud screeching shrill! Harris fires and holds the beam on the creature until it disintegrates! The Ebulliti is gone and Khalid is alive along with his brother, but Khalid will never be the same. He will never be able to live a normal life. He will never play basketball again.

With the young boy in his arms, he took a look through the house only to discover that the mother was dead from a knife wound to the chest. The large carving knife was still stuck in her chest, apparently from Khalid before he rejected the Ebulliti. The Ebulliti with nowhere else to go would have found its way into the young boy if Harris had not killed it.

Harris was headed to the next victim's house when he got an alert from his partner Tyler. Harris alerted the proper authorities about the incident at the Morris home. Other than Khalid's tragedy, the boy's lives are no longer in danger.

The guardians are able to communicate with each other telepathically. Tyler had just informed Harris that Kyle had eaten human flesh and that the transformation had already started.

Chapter 35

Nalanni's body temperature had subsided. She was feeling better now but remained quiet. She had just envisioned Kyle devouring the girl retainer. The flashes of the grotesque images flashed in her mind and she realized the urgency of her task. I tried to talk to her to ask her who was coming. I asked her over and over and she just sat there staring into nothing. Her eyes remained open and her pupils were as large as dimes. Kendra looked at me with a solemn look on her face. She felt that Nalanni needed to rest. Paris was standing next to or sort of behind Kendra. Paris steps up around Kendra and says, "She thinks she needs to go to him before he comes for her." I turned back to look at Paris. Her eyes were as wide as Nalanni's. She too was now staring into nothing. She repeated one more time, "She needs to go to him before he comes for her." But this time with more conviction in her voice.

"Who's coming for her?! I asked Paris.

She repeats it again, "She needs to go to him now before he comes for her!"

"Where do we need to go and who are we going to?" I asked desperately.

Then Nalanni answered, "He's at the theater now. He wants to come for me. He wants to come for me but he can't. We need to go to him now!"

My heart felt like it was about to bust through my chest. I started to panic. I yelled, "What theater?!"

Paris spoke up saying, "The one over there." making a pointing jester in the south west direction.

Everybody panicking now except Nalanni and Paris. We all looked at each other confused. As everybody blurted out theaters in the south west direction, I asked Nalanni in a calm voice, "Where is the theater baby?"

As if she had come out of the trans, she turns to me and says in a calm voice, "The old one by the donut shop."

I thought to myself, *"by the donut shop? What theater? What donut shop?* Then it hit me. The Winchell's on Manchester. But the 5th Avenue has been closed for over twenty years. I was questioning the thought in my head. Kendra looks at me and says, "What?" She knew by the look on my face that I had figured it out but was not sure. While I was still pondering the thought in my head Nalanni says, "That's it. We need to get there now! We are wasting time!"

Damon puts a gun in the back of his pants and one in his waist and says, "Come on bro, let's go get this mutha fucka! He's not getting my niece!"

"Those won't stop him. I can stop him but we need to go now before its complete." said Nalanni.

"Before what's complete baby?"

"We need to go, he's getting stronger!"

"Ok let's go but you're not going. You have to stay here, it's too dangerous for you!"

"Daddy I can stop him, but we gotta go now."

"No! I'm not going to let anything happen to you!"

I told Kendra to keep an eye on Nalanni and Paris. Damon and I rushed out the door headed to the old 5th Avenue Theater on Manchester Blvd.

Chapter 36

Feeling that he was out of danger of being seen, Tyler came out of the shed. It was now dark outside. He had quickly hidden inside the shed to keep from being seen by the male retainer. Hearing the door open and not closing immediately gave way to the thought that the male retainer was looking for him and might look over the wall that he had hidden behind. Being seen at this time was not an option, for that would surely cause alarm to Kyle's retainers and ruin the idea of a sneak attack and get him killed. Tyler crept over to the wall. Not sure of what he would see, he peeked over the wall to see several retainers going inside the old theater. There had to be at least two dozen or more. He knew he was out numbered, so for now he had to stay out of sight.

Harris reached the house on eighty third street just minutes after Damon and I had left. He was surprised that Nalanni was still there at the house. He knew that we had no chance of taking down Kyle and his retainer protectors. He also knew we would be out matched and overpowered. Kyle was getting stronger by the second. Even if his transformation was not complete we didn't have a chance to defeat him without Nalanni. He knew we needed Nalanni with us so he was going to get her there even if I didn't want her there.

I had no idea that what I was about to encounter was extremely more powerful and deadlier than I could have imagined. Nalanni knew, and so did Harris.

We pulled up to the theater slowly. We decided to circle the building to scope it out. The alley would be the most direct way of circling the theater without wasting much time. We made a right on 5th avenue heading north. Everything looked quiet so far. We reached the alley and everything was still clear. Then out of nowhere comes Tyler. I almost hit him with the truck. Tyler jumped out of nowhere right in front of my blazer. He cautioned me not to stop as to not arouse suspicion. He ran alongside the blazer down the alley until he was out of sight of anyone that may look out the back door. We exited the alley on 3rd avenue and made a right turn and parked next to the check cashing place which was directly across the street from the Cream Crop Bakery. Tyler filled us in on what was going on. He told us that there were two dozen or more retainers inside the theater now. We were outnumbered and out powered, but we had to take him down now Nalanni told us. The crazy thing is we don't know who or what "HE" is. Tyler sat in the Blazer looking confused. He was looking around as if we had forgotten something. Damon and I both noticed his confused look. Damon asked, "What the hell is wrong with you?"

Tyler asked, "Where is the girl, Nalanni?"

I quickly answered with much anger in my voice, "She's not here!"

"We cannot do this without her. He'll be too strong for just us." said Tyler.

"But she's just a little girl! My little girl!"

"You under estimate her. She's more powerful than you think. The sooner you realize it, the better off you will all be."

I couldn't grasp the idea of putting my baby girl in danger and was not going to let anyone else do it either.

I told Tyler that we had no choice because my daughter was not going to be here and it was up to me to keep her safe. I didn't want to hear anything else about it. I put the truck in gear and proceeded to the theater. This was it. We were about to engage "Him."

Chapter 37

Harris knew we needed Nalanni if we were going to be successful in defeating Kyle. He knew as well as Nalanni that Kyle had fed on human flesh and was getting stronger by the second. She knew we had no chance against Kyle without her. She had never actually known her mother and was not going to lose her father to a creature that she was here to protect the world from.

Harris went in the house and told Kendra, "I need the girl to come with me."

Kendra being protective of Nalanni said, "She's not going anywhere with you! Her father would kill you if he knew you were here trying to take her and put her in harm's way." Kendra's voice was filled with anger and much needed emphasis on her decision to keep Nalanni there with her. Just then Nalanni said, "Kendra I need to go. My dad and uncle Damon can't defeat him without me. They will fail and failing is not an option when it comes to my family."

She had delivered the statement with so much conviction and maturity. Kendra had briefly forgotten that she was only five years old. Kendra looked Nalanni in the eyes and Nalanni said to her, "Don't worry I'll be alright," without even moving her lips. Nalanni had just communicated with Kendra telepathically. Kendra just looked at Nalanni and said, "Ok, I know you will."

Although Paris wanted to go, she knew

Nalanni didn't need her there, so she stayed home with Kendra.

We pulled up to the theater once more. I decided to park down the alley next to the building, but I left enough room to exit and reenter from both sides of the truck. I left enough room for cars to pass through the alley. I got out of the truck and walked around to the back and pulled out one of the flame guns that we had gotten from Sidewinder. Tyler asked what it was and I told him it was a flame gun. He said it would prove to be effective, but only to the retainers, but not on "Him." We walked up to the back door of the theater to find the door unlocked. We were either lucky or walking into a trap. Damon pulled out his 10mm and chambered the first round. Tyler noticed and said that bullets will not hurt him, only make him madder. Damon said we'll see about that. Tyler then tells Damon, "It may be useful on the others, but it will only slow them down, not kill them.
Once inside, there was a long hallway with four doors, two on each side. It was mildly dark inside so we stayed close together. I led the way with Damon bringing up the rear. We knew from Tyler's observation that there were several retainers inside. It was dark and very quiet. We moved slowly toward the first door which was on our right. The old theater smelled of mildew and dust.

I crossed the entrance of the first door and stopped on the far side. We didn't know what awaited us on the other side of the door. Were there several retainers inside waiting to pounce on us as we walked through the door? Will we be able to fight them off if attacked? How strong or fast were they? All of these questions breezed through my head as I contemplated opening the door. We are here now no need to get scared now. My baby girl's safety is a stake. I told the guys that we would go on the count of three. I counted down, "One.. Two.. Three" I pushed opened the door quickly! There was nothing inside but boxes. The room was dark but Tyler's light helped us see. Damon stayed at the door making sure no one could sneak up behind us. I called out, "This room is clear."

We exited that room and moved on to the next door. It appeared to be a cross sectioned corridor at the end of the hall. Damon was now in the front. He had his gun up and ready. I knew it would not stop the retainers but it could slow them down until I could flame them. We reached the next door. This time Damon crossed the door to the other side. I stood against the opposite wall but slightly to the right to give myself room to flame whatever came running out. Damon opened the door on the count of three just as before. One, two, three! Door opened! Nothing was in there. It was totally empty. Two doors down and two doors to go. I took the lead again. Damon picked up the rear.

All of a sudden Damon says, "Oh SHIT!"

I said "What happen?!"

Damon said, "I saw something!"

"What did you see?" said Tyler.

"I don't know what the hell it was but I know I saw something flash across the hall into the second door!"

We needed to go back and check it out. I led the way with the flame gun ready to blaze. We slowly crept back towards the second door which was on our right. My heart was beating like a jackhammer. I was sure we closed the door when we left the first time. Now it was open. Who or what had opened it. We were about to find out. I got to the door, peeked inside over my right shoulder. Nothing was visible. This is the room that was totally empty. The room was dark. The only light showing in was the little light from the hallway behind us, which was very little. I noticed something that was definitely not there the first time. I called out, "Hey, who's in here?" I took a couple of slow calculated steps towards the shadowy figure. It appeared to be a person kneeling down. As I got closer the figure stood up. "SHIT!" I jumped back. The figure moved towards us slowly. Tyler said in a strong voice, "Flame it now!"

I didn't. In a flash it did something that I

wasn't expecting. It lunged at me! "OH SHIT!"

POW! Damon fired a single shot to the head! It was a retainer. It fell back and down to the floor. The shot was right in the forehead, blowing off most of the back of a female retainer's skull. She lay there for about 5 seconds and starts to get up. Tyler says, "Flame her now!"

VROOSH, goes the flame gun setting the retainer on fire. She lets out a shrilling scream and burst into flames and turns to ashes in seconds. The ashes extinguish dissipated almost immediately.

How did we miss her? Where did she come from?

Damon confused and in disbelief wonders how could a person's head get blown off and they still get up? What the fuck are we dealing with?

His face looking worried and filled with fear, now doubts their ability to defeat them and especially "Him".

Chapter 38

Outside the old theater Harris was pulling up with Nalanni. Nalanni knew what she had to do. She knew she had to confront and defeat Kyle Massey. She also knew that she was the only one that could do it, and she was ready for the task. It's amazing how a five year old could become so serious and focused. She was committed and confident to the task of defeating Kyle. Harris had no doubt that Nalanni would succeed. They approached the door. When they got within five feet of the door it opened. Nalanni had opened the door with her mind. Her telekinetic powers had increased profusely. As she stepped inside the door way, the lights in the hall lit up with every step. She appeared to be gliding instead of walking. The hallway was lit up with light all the way to the end.

Having made it through the hall way, we came to the main corridor that leads to the theater show room. The theater had been gutted out. There were absolutely no seats inside the theater. Other than the retainer we torched, we hadn't seen a single one. The cold cement floor of the theater still sloped down to the stage. The theater was dimly lit, but the stage was dark. We took a few more steps toward the stage. There was something down there next to the stage. It was fairly large. It just sat there, not moving, not making a sound, but watching us watch it. We kept moving. We were now in the middle of the theater. Before we knew it there were retainers at every exit. They just stood there. There numbers were increasing. Three came in then 5, 6, 7, and 10. Before we knew it they had completely surrounded us. There were at least three dozen or more of them. I thought about flaming them with the flame gun but I knew there was no way to get all of them. I flicked on the flame. The flame went out and wouldn't remain lit so I continued to try to light it several times. They closed in on us leaving one path, and that path was to what was standing next to the stage. If they decided to rush us now we would be over run in a matter of seconds.

They came closer to us as if herding us to the large figure. We were forced to take several steps forward. The large figure was breathing loud and vigorously. We came within about fifteen feet of the large thing. It was cloaked and hooded. We couldn't tell if it were a man, animal, or combination of both. We stood there and stared in fear, wondering what was under the cloak and hood. I stood there thinking, "Is this "Him"? It looked more like an it than a who. We heard some commotion coming from behind us. The noise was coming from the same direction we had just come through. The noise seemed to be getting closer. At first I thought I was the only one that heard it. Then I saw Damon sort of responded to the disruptive sounds coming from behind us and getting closer. Damon had a look on his face like, "What the hell is that"? The large thing started moving towards us slowly. It was still in the shadows of the large vacant theater. It seemed to grow with every step. It must be about seven feet tall. Its eyes were a bright glowing orange. It took a couple more steps into the light. We still couldn't make out what it was because of the cloak. Damon said, "FUCK THIS SHIT!" and fired two rounds into what should have been its chest. The beast or whatever it was let out a loud roar. (*ROOAR!*) It stretched out its arms, the cloak flew off and fell to the ground. All at once we tried to jump back but the retainers wouldn't permit us to go anywhere. A retainer had already knocked the gun out of Damon's hand. The gun had fallen to the floor and was lost in the crowd. Damon reached for his spare gun. One of the male retainers grabbed it as he reached for it.

I was shoved from the back toward the creature. Its long muscular arms swung around and struck me across the right side of my face sending me flying into the crowd of retainers. I found myself on the once chair filled, cold theater floor looking up at this hulking creature. The horrifying creature looked to be nearly eight feet tall now. Its head was very large and protruded out at its brow line. Its teeth were rowed like that of a shark. The grotesque creature snarled and continued to breathe heavily as it drooled at the idea that it would be feeding on our warm flesh soon. I slowly sat up in an upright position on the floor. The once carpeted floor was cold and felt damp. Retainers were all around me but left a clear view for the creature to see me. I couldn't see Damon or Tyler from where I was on the floor. The retainers on the sides of me made room for the creature to approach me. I looked up at it. It was closer than I thought it would be. It felt like it knocked me about 20 feet away when it slugged me. But I was only about ten feet from it. Damn it's ugly! I couldn't believe I was seeing this thing with my own two eyes. These kinds of things

only exist in the movies, not in real life. I
had just rapped my mind around everything
that has been going on, and now this.

I could hear Damon yelling somewhere
behind me, "Yal mutha fuckas let me go!" It
sounded like he was struggling to get away
from his captors. But more was going on
behind me than Damon struggling with the
retainers that were holding him. Something
serious was going on back there and it was
getting closer. All I could think of was,
WHAT NOW?

Chapter 39

Nalanni was making her way down the corridor with James Harris closely behind her. The stench of the torched retainer still fills the air. Although she smells the burnt flesh it didn't detour her from the mission she had now set out to accomplish. She knew she had to be there to save her dad because he and the others had no chance without her. Her powers are getting stronger with each passing minute. Powers that she would soon have to call upon for her family's survival as well as her own.

Retainers were coming out of the wood works. Nalanni had gotten so strong that she only needed to look at them and they would go flying out of her way. Pushing them into walls would not stop them but merely clear her way. At one point two young adult retainers that couldn't have been no older than twenty years old attempted to rush her. They ran at her with malicious intent. Nalanni just raised her right hand like a traffic control officer signaling for cars to stop. That simple gesture delivered a massive surge of energy that literally stripped the Ebulliti's life force from the retainer's bodies. Nalanni's energy blast was so strong, the human aspect of them was unable to survive. The bodies appeared to look normal but lacked life, as if their souls had been ripped away. She had not learned how to save the lives of the people the Ebulliti imprinted on yet.

Her powers were coming to her at an alarming speed, which proved to be beneficial and potentially dangerous. She had not had time to use most of her powers. She was learning to use them as circumstances permitted use of them. She has these powers, but she doesn't know where they are coming from.

She knows she has the power to do things the moment the power is manifested within her. The moment the power is manifested in her, she becomes aware of them and knows automatically when or if she needs to use them. Her powers are about to be tested as well as her ability to use them. To save her father and the others she's going to need to exercise them at their highest degree.

Nalanni moved through the corridor with a purpose. He focus had become heightened.

She knows she can't fail and was starting to know that she won't fail. The child in her has been locked deep inside. This is not the time for the child in her to surface. That could mean the death of the others as well as her.

What use to be Kyle Massey, won't show any remorse to Nalanni. It'll kill her whether she's in child form or not. The creature knows its survival along with all the other Ebulliti's survival depends on it.

She's getting closer to the main theater room. The lighting is dimming slowly and she is moving faster now. No more retainers have tried to attack her. James Harris is following behind her closely with his flashlight looking weapon. The weapon had proved to be effective earlier tonight and he was counting on it again right now, at this very moment.

He was able to successfully eradicate nineteen earlier. There are several more out there that need to be taken care of. They are small fish in this big pond, and we are trying to take down the big fish right now. Kyle Massey was the big fish, and a big fish he was.

Chapter 40

Kyle Massey approached me slowly, snarling, and drooling from the mouth. Its monstrous face was a pale green. It shined like it was glazed with an oil of some kind. It had pants that had been ripped because of its size. Its chest was wide and shiny as well. It took a few more steps closer to me. Its mouth was big enough to swallow a small basketball. The head had to be huge for that mouth to fit on that ugly face.

It had its eyes set on me like I was the main course. The creature had gotten so close to me that I could now smell its stench. It was horrible. It was like a landfill. For a second I thought I was going to vomit. I managed to keep my partially digested food down.

The retainers stood by quietly. They seem to be waiting on their master's next move. They knew that it was about to eat me, right here, right now.

Damon had stopped struggling behind me. Even the commotion back behind me stopped. All was still and quiet except the creature. It still crept towards me. It got to within about four feet of me. It reached to me opening its mouth wide. I knew I was dead.

Nalanni was at the entrance to the main theater. She could not see her father but she knew he was in the theater. There are about 40 retainers in the theater, or maybe more. No one had noticed her yet. All the action was going on down by the stage. There is a crowd of retainers standing near the stage, all facing the hulking creature.

James Harris swings to the right to flank the crowd. Nalanni comes in and straight to the crowd. Nobody had noticed her. Nalanni is coming to finally face Kyle Massey!

My heart was beating deep, hard, and fast. I thought I would wake from this very bad nightmare any second. This was no dream and I was not sleep. I thought about closing my eyes in hope that it would be over quickly. I would have never thought in a million years that I would go out like this. Damn! This is it!

Tyler broke free and jumped in front of me

just as the creature reached down to grab me. It caught the creature by surprise but didn't alter is momentum. It grabbed Tyler. Its large hands wrapped around his body in a tight grip. It picked up Tyler, and in a single bite, bit off Tyler's head at the neck.

Blood squirted out his body at the shoulders and oozed out the creature's mouth as it lets out another loud roar.

I was soaked in Tyler's blood as it squirted out of Tyler's body and all over me. The creature stood directly over me, chewing Tyler's head. Tyler's skull crunching and cracking in its mouth like a big peanut M&M. With each chew blood continued to drip on me.

Tyler's lifeless corps fell to the ground beside me. It would have fell on me, had I not rolled over. The creature chewed and chewed, then stopped and looked over me past the crowd. Something had caught its attention.

Chapter 41

Nalanni saw Kyle bite the head off Tyler, killing him instantly. The gory action had no effect on the five year old. No ordinary child could have handled this kind of horrific scene. Nalanni was no ordinary child. Nalanni just watched.

The retainers turned to her as their master noticed her. He stopped chewing and starred at her. His time to kill and feast on her flesh was here.

Immediately an eight foot lane opened up to allow Kyle to get to Nalanni. It was like somebody counted the retainers and split them in half.

Half way down the lane to the left was Damon being held by two young, large male retainers. Her father was down closer to the stage near Kyle. Still on the floor he turned and saw his baby girl.

My eyes widened with fear. My heart seemed to beat in loud, slow pounding beats. It was like my worst nightmare was being played out right before my eyes. My fear had me glued to the floor. I could not move. Everything was moving in slow motion, but happening too fast for me to react in a way that would save my daughter. Tears welled up in my eyes.

I thought fear had me glued to the floor but it was the retainers that were holding me there. I tried to get up but they were holding me down there. I yelled for her to get out of here, but she didn't budge.

Now all the retainer's eyes were on her. She needed to free her family so they could get out of the way.

Nalanni looked at the crowd on the left then to the right in a slow but deliberate motion of her head. She held up both hands towards each half of the crowd. A bright, blue, steady light beamed from her palms. The light was bright like that of a flash from a camera. The retainers stood there and moaned as the light seemed to go right through their bodies. Then FLASH! The light intensified ten times brighter for a fraction of a second then it was gone. All the retainers fell out on conscious but alive.

I realized I was free. I rushed over to grab my flame gun, lit the fuse and VROOSH! I set that ugly mother fucker on fire. I was not going to let it get my baby girl. I didn't care what kind of powers she has.

The creature went up in flames! Damon dove on the floor and grabbed his gun and unloaded the remainder of his clip into the creature's chest and head. The creature stood there burning and roaring loudly! Then it did something that we could not believe. It sort of flexed its muscles and the flames extinguished. I said, "WHAT IN HELL?" I quickly tried to torch it again. VROOSH, but nothing happened. Again, VROOSH, still nothing happened. The creature had become fire proof. The creature stood there smoldering. The smoldering didn't last for long. When it finished, there was not a burn on it at all. It even excreted the bullets out of its head and body. I thought to myself, "Nalanni."

Nalanni knew all those weapons would not hurt Kyle. She knew what she had to do. She need to get close to him, actually she needed to touch him.

Kyle felt his time was at hand. He's close to achieving his objective of killing Nalanni and taking the life of my baby girl. Once done, the Ebulliti could take over the earth and heard the humans like cattle and raid the earth of all its natural resources. Mission complete. The earth would belong to them and we would be made their food until all the humans were dead and all the earth's natural resources were depleted.

Nalanni knew what their plans were and was not going to let it happen. She needs to get to him now. She starts to glide towards Kyle. He starts to take large steps towards her. Nalanni's glide is smooth and straight forward. But as she gets close to him, she starts to change.

Kyle does not notice the change in her or does not care. He keeps stepping forward with the steps getting faster.

Nalanni's skin starts to turn a light violet color and her eyes darken. She appeared to be on fire from the inside.

They meet. Kyle grabs her as he did Tyler.

Knowing what had just happened to Tyler, I let out a large yell, "NOOOOO!"

Kyle opens his mouth and lifts her towards it. Damon, as well as I thought this was the end of my baby. I couldn't stand there and watch, so I ran at it and as I got close Nalanni telepathically tells me to stop, and to not get any closer. I heard her voice tell me in my head, "Stop daddy, I got this. Trust me."

I stopped. Damon yells at me, "What are you doing? Don't let that thing eat my niece!" He starts to charge the creature too. I stopped him by grabbing him and tackling him to the ground. I tell him, "She'll be alright, just wait."

Just when Kyle thought he was about to

succeed and feed on Nalanni's flesh, she takes both her hands and grabs the sides of his big head. The creature stops taking her to his mouth. Nalanni's pupils enlarge to completely fill the iris of her eyes. Her hands start to glow blue and she stares the creature dead smack in its eyes. Her stare becomes so powerful the creature's powerful roar is reduced to a growl of pain. The creature starts to shake violently. Damon and I can do nothing but look on as Nalanni takes on a powerful creature ten times her size. Although I was watching the whole ordeal, I was still afraid for my daughter's life.

Kyle's growls are now reduced to animal cries of pain. He starts to vibrate as the light within her gets brighter and brighter. Her hands blue glow is so bright now that we can barely stand to look.

BOOM! Kyle's body explodes with a burst of light that was so bright that it blinded us for several seconds.

When I got my sight back Nalanni lay there on the floor not moving at all. I ran over to her, she's not moving. I checked her pulse and she has no pulse. This time instead of welling up in my eyes, tears stream down my face. No, No, No not my baby! Kneeling down on my knees, I start to cry. I cry out all the things I could have done to stop her. I pick her up to my chest holding her tight. I lost my baby! She's gone. I failed!

Just then something strange started to happen. A bright light was shining above us coming down from the ceiling. We had no idea what was happening now because there were no light fixtures on the ceiling of the theater. It was ghostly and glowing bright. Like a large glowing bubble floating down towards us. It descended on us. As it got closer, it started taking the shape of a person. We got worried. We thought the ordeal wasn't over. Damon reloaded his gun and aimed it at the ghostly figure. I put Nalanni down, picked up the flame gun, and lit the fuse. We were about to fire, then it said, "Keith, put down the weapons, it's over now." I knew that voice, but it couldn't be. Tears started to well up in my eyes again. The image became clear. It was Nakol. More tears came rushing out of my eyes. I asked how could this be? She said, "Our baby needs me now. Don't worry she'll be ok."

"I failed her. I was suppose to take care of her."

I cried to her like a baby. I had just let our baby girl get killed.

She kneeled down on the other side of Nalanni, put her hand on her face and said, "She's just a little tired. My sweet baby girl is stronger than you think. You underestimate her."

Nakol bends down closer to her and whispers in her ear, "You've down well my baby, now it's time to wake up. Breathe now baby."

Just then Nalanni takes in a deep breath, and starts to breathe. I hug my baby. She looks up and says, "Daddy, I heard mommy talking to me."

"Hi baby."

"Mommy! You came back to us!"

"No baby, I just came back to make sure you're alright. Mommy can't stay but mommy loves you and your sister very much."

My five year old daughter had defeated a large hulking creature ten times her size without even a whimper. But seeing her mother here for the first time, she starts to cry like the little vulnerable five year old child she really is.

"Mommy why do you have to leave again?"

"Baby, mommy can't explain it right now, but you will understand all this one day baby, I promise."

Nakol tells me to make sure Nalanni and Paris go everywhere together from now on, and that they should never be apart. She made me promise. She said good bye to us and rises up and fades away. Nalanni and I hold each other tightly. Damon comes in and joins us in partial, family group hug.

James Harris walks into the theater, all the retainers start to wake up slowly. They don't know what happened to them or how they got there. Harris new if he had stayed in the theater he would have been knocked unconscious also and would no longer be a guardian. His job is far from over, so he could not allow himself to be destroyed.

Nalanni and Paris will be tested. Their need for each other will grow. The two of them will have to depend on each other in their near futures for their survival and safety.

But for now the threat was over and Nalanni could go home and get some much needed rest.